COUNCIL OF PATRIOTS

8/19

Help us Rate this book…
Put your initials on the
Left side and your rating
on the right side.
1 = Didn't care for
2 = It was O.K.
3 = It was great

DATE DUE

AUG 2 3 2019 (MRH)			
OCT 2 1 2019			
NOV 3 0 2019			
MAR 1 6 2020			

MRH — 1 2 ③
TP — 1 2 ③
_____ 1 2 3
_____ 1 2 3
_____ 1 2 3
_____ 1 2 3
_____ 1 2 3
_____ 1 2 3
_____ 1 2 3
_____ 1 2 3
_____ 1 2 3
_____ 1 2 3
_____ 1 2 3
_____ 1 2 3
_____ 1 2 3

PRINTED IN U.S.A.

Council of Patriots

Book 2 of the *Corps Justice* Series

Author: C. G. Cooper

www.CorpsJustice.com

Warning: *This story is intended for mature audiences and contains profanity and violence.*

Dedications

To my amazing wife who never tires of proofing my writing. I love you, K, and couldn't do it without you!

To my entire family and amazing group of friends that have supported me so unconditionally. You guys are awesome.

Chapter 1
Washington, D.C.
10:35am, September 11th

CONGRESSMAN ZIMMER KNEW he was in deep shit. The last six months replayed in his mind as he swirled the remnants of his fifth drink. Ever since the episode in Las Vegas, his life had drastically changed. He remembered the incident like it was yesterday. Hell, he'd relived it every night in his dreams. He hadn't had one decent night's rest.

✦✦✦

Six months earlier, Brandon Zimmer, a promising first-term United States representative from

Massachusetts, was on the rise. Barely thirty years old, Zimmer was no novice in the political world. He'd first accompanied his parents on the campaign trail as a newborn. His father, U.S. Senator Richard Zimmer of Massachusetts, employed young Brandon over the years in positions ranging from runner to assistant campaign manager.

After graduating from an elite private school, Brandon matriculated to the Ivy League. His father, a Harvard alum, pushed for his son to follow his lead. Brandon decided to rebel and go to Yale instead. He did attend Harvard for his MBA, however.

During his years in school Brandon excelled in academics and always elected to be part of the student council. Yes, politics was in his blood.

A year prior, Congressman Brandon Zimmer won the vacated congressional seat in his home district in Massachusetts. Despite being a staunch Democrat in a very blue state, he narrowly won. The early campaign looked promising and his staff expected a landslide victory. Zimmer had the good looks the media loved. He was also the son of a long-standing and extremely popular Senator.

Despite his status and the endorsement of his six-term father in the Senate, Brandon's playboy ways were soon splashed throughout social media. Pictures of Zimmer dancing with naked coeds at a Mardi Gras bash in New Orleans the year before almost sealed his fate. Soon other reports, photos and videos surfaced. It was only through the damage control of his staff and his father's wealthy backers that he was able to win the election.

After the fiasco, his father put his foot down.

"Son, this is your last shot. I will not come to your rescue again. You've got to learn to control your urges. Do you really want to give up everything we've worked for?"

Although he'd promised to leave his partying days behind, halfway into his first year as Congressman, Zimmer accepted the invitation of a small Japanese lobbyist who represented the gaming industry. Brandon first met Ishi Nakamura at Harvard Business School. They'd worked hard and played even harder. After graduation Zimmer entered politics and Nakamura entered the family gaming business in Las Vegas. They'd kept in touch over the years and always promised to visit.

Not long after Zimmer was sworn in he received a call from his friend. Ishi wanted to offer his congratulations and let Brandon know that he was now heading up his father's small lobbying firm, Ichiban Gaming. Brandon was honestly excited for his friend and mentioned that they should link up sometime soon.

Six months later, he received another call from Ishi.

"Hey, brother. Just wanted to let you know that we're having a couple of your peers out here in a week to show them around. Didn't know if you might like to join them. You could make some new friends and I can give you a tour of Sin City," Ishi invited.

Brandon moaned before answering. "I don't know. I'm on a pretty short leash around here."

"Come on. What happened to the Brandon that used to sneak weed into Professor Flannigan's lectures?"

The freshman Congressman chuckled, "I'm a member of the House now, Ishi. Being in the wrong place at the wrong time already bit me once."

"I know, I know. I'm just giving you a hard time. Look, consider it payback for all those times you hooked me up with your rejects. I promise to wine you and dine you and nothing else."

Brandon took a second to respond. What could it hurt? "Well, as long as we stick to food, shows and a little gambling...I guess I can go."

✛ ✛ ✛

Congressman Zimmer wished he'd said no. The trip started out like any other fact-finding junket. Lectures and meetings followed by expensive dinners and more meetings. It all fell apart for Zimmer on the third night.

After a long day hobnobbing with local gaming contacts, Brandon needed a break. He slipped away and headed back to the swanky new hotel-casino, Zeitaku, owned by one of Ishi's clients. Ducking into one of the many bars he'd toured earlier in the week, he soon found a dark corner and made himself at home.

Halfway into his third martini, a gorgeous blonde walked into the almost deserted bar. *Wow. Look at the body on that one.*

She sat down at the bar and ordered a drink from the Japanese bartender. After a couple sips from her cocktail her eyes wandered around the nearly empty bar. Almost squinting, she caught Brandon's eye. She smiled sheepishly and went back to her drink.

Five minutes later the young woman walked towards the restroom but veered over to the Congressman's alcove.

"I'm sorry. I don't mean to bother you, but are you by any chance Congressman Zimmer?" she asked shyly.

It wasn't every day that Zimmer was recognized in public, but his ego always loved it.

He plastered on his best man-of-the-people-smile. "Yes I am."

The blonde smiled ecstatically. "I thought so! Do you mind if I sit down?"

Brandon gestured to the other seat. "Please."

Her name was Beth. She was also from the East Coast, and had gone to the University of North Carolina at Chapel Hill. They hit it off immediately after ribbing each other about the strength of their alma maters' basketball teams. Zimmer conceded that UNC was a perennial powerhouse on the court. His concession made Beth beam with pride.

They stayed in the bar until it closed, drinking countless martinis in the process. One thing led to another and the pair eventually made it back to Zimmer's penthouse suite.

The next thing Zimmer remembered was waking up with his face cradled in Beth's perfect breasts. He felt severely hung-over, but that was nothing new. *Must have been a really good night*, he thought.

Something felt strange as he started to move. He didn't remember getting into any kinky jello stuff, but his hands and midsection felt sticky.

His eyes were still blurry and he could just make out Beth's peaceful face. Man was she sleeping hard. He pushed himself off her naked body, looked down, and screamed.

Everything came into stark focus. Beth's beautiful body was completely dismembered. Her arms and legs had been cut off. A huge amount of blood was soaking the king-size mattress. Still screaming he looked down at himself and saw that he was covered in blood as well. Even worse, he raised his hands to his face and realized that his right hand held a long serrated knife, caked with congealing, sticky blood.

He screamed once more and fainted.

When he came to, hotel security staff was wandering around the bedroom. All were Japanese. They'd apparently wrapped him in a robe but neglected to clean off any of Beth's blood. He started to panic as he took in the scene. Beth's body was barely visible because it was surrounded by camera-wielding security crew. He even noticed one man casually taking videos of the room.

The cameraman noticed Zimmer awake and motioned to one of the other men. The man nodded and headed towards the fallen congressman.

The security guard walked over to Brandon and addressed him in heavily accented English. "Congressman Zimmer, I am head of hotel security. Would it be possible to take your statement now?"

Brandon didn't know how to answer. Was he going to jail? What the hell was happening?

"I'd like to call my attorney first," he forced out with as much conviction as he could muster.

The head of security nodded. "I understand, Congressman. However, this is a highly sensitive issue. I would recommend cooperating with us. Failure to do so could make the situation much worse."

"What do you mean by that?"

"Let me just say that you would not want these videos to get leaked to the police or the public."

Brandon's head started to clear as did his bravado. "Are you trying to frame me?"

The security man looked almost contrite and bowed before answering. "Of course not, Congressman. You do see our dilemma..."

He was interrupted by Ishi Nakamura bursting through the door.

"What is the meaning of this?!"

The guard bowed in deference. "Nakamura-san, I did not know that you were acquainted with the Congressman."

Ishi looked enraged. "Of course I am, you idiot. Does Mr. Saito know about this?"

"He does. Saito-san wanted me to take care of this personally."

Ishi calmed and replied, "Tell him that I am here and wish to speak with him."

The head of security bowed and stepped outside to make the call.

Ishi turned to his friend. "What the hell happened, Brandon?"

Brandon's composure slipped as he answered, "I...I...I don't know. Last thing I remember I was having a great time with this girl, and then I wake up straddling a corpse. What the fuck, man?!"

Ishi put a sympathetic hand on his friend's shoulder. "Calm down. I'll take care of this."

"How the hell are you gonna take care of this?! They've got my prints all over and they keep taking pictures!"

Ishi paused and looked squarely at Brandon. "Do you trust me?"

Still panicking, Zimmer couldn't think of anything else to say. "I...I guess."

Shaking his head Ishi scolded, "That's not good enough. Do you trust me?"

Brandon looked at his old friend momentarily, then nodded. "Yes I trust you."

The corner of Ishi's mouth turned up in sly grin. "OK. This won't be easy, but I may be able to call in a few favors. The owner of this hotel, Mr. Saito, is a client of my firm and a friend of my father. Let me see what I can do."

Now in tears, Brandon pleaded, "Do whatever you have to and get me out of this, Ishi."

That was six months earlier. At the time all he wanted was to be out of that bloody room. Congressman Zimmer never had time to think about the consequences. Little did he know how much that favor would cost.

Chapter 2
Turks and Caicos, Providenciales Island
9:00am, September 13th

CAL STRETCHED LAZILY on the king-size bed and looked across the huge suite. Neil was still monitoring the surveillance cameras. They'd been in Turks for just over a week, and had taken full advantage of the local amenities. That fact was clearly illustrated by the massive headache threatening to overtake Cal's attention.

Cal snapped his fingers at Neil. "Anything new?"

Not looking up from the monitor, the genius known as Neil Patel answered, "Nope. Our boy is still sleeping off his hangover."

"I feel like I should be doing the same thing."

Neil chuckled and looked back at his friend through his stylish Prada glasses. "You were pretty funny when Brian dragged you back in here last night. What the hell did you get into?"

Cal rubbed his hands over his eyes. "I was the idiot that thought he could match Master Sergeant Trent drink for drink."

MSgt Willy Trent was an enormous man. Standing just under seven feet with the physique of an NFL linebacker, Trent was a hard man to miss. He and Cal were both former Marines and competed in anything and everything possible. There was only one problem. Despite the fact that Cal was a very fit five foot ten former grunt and a deadly warrior, not many people could match Trent's athletic abilities.

Cal changed the subject, not wanting to make his headache even worse. "When does my shift start?"

"It's nine o'clock now. You're not on until eleven." Neil went back to his vigil and coffee.

Cal tried to shake the cobwebs. "Sweet. That gives me some time to marinate under a nice hot shower."

"You need it. You smell like a brewery," Neil answered sniffing the air.

Cal gave his friend a middle-finger salute and trudged off to the bathroom. As he soaked in the shower, his mind drifted. He thought about his entrance into his deceased father's company, Stokes Security International (SSI). Had it really been a year since he'd started working at SSI?

It seemed like only yesterday that he had accepted the position as head of SSI's covert division. His cousin, Travis Haden, was CEO of SSI and a former SEAL. He'd not only enticed Cal into taking the position, but had also allowed the former Marine to utilize SSI assets to avenge his fiancé's murder.

Cal had exacted his revenge in the gang leader's underground lair, not far from SSI's headquarters, Camp Spartan, just south of Nashville, Tennessee. It was a close fight (Cal had the scars to prove it), but he'd finally killed the criminal who'd taken his beloved Jessica's life.

He still felt the bitter sting of grief. It had lessened over time, but Cal still couldn't bring himself to start dating again. His friends knew it would happen in time, but no one pushed the issue.

Cal remembered Jessica's funeral. It was a beautiful ceremony on a bright sunny day. They'd buried her on the grounds of Camp Spartan, and Cal often took a jog up to her grave. He liked to think that Jess was now watching over him as he continued his journey with SSI.

After the funeral, Travis had introduced him to the men that would completely change his life's path: the Council of Patriots.

+ + +

The Council was comprised of nine men. All were former U.S. political leaders, including three former Presidents, four senators and two congressmen. All were Republicans except for former President Hank Waller, a Democrat.

He remembered that first meeting vividly. They'd each introduced themselves then told him the story of their formation.

The Council had formed in the early 2000's after the disaster of 9/11. It all started with a couple of former political opponents playing 18 holes at the Army-Navy Country Club just outside of D.C. Both men were former presidents. Hank Waller was a two-term Democrat from California, and John Kelton was a single-term Republican from Tennessee. They'd been bitter rivals for years, but the presidency has a way of broadening perspectives. Waller and Kelton had collaborated on various relief efforts after their presidencies, and grew to respect one another. They'd become close friends despite their political leanings.

It was on that chilly May morning in Arlington that the two former presidents first conferred about the threats affecting the United States. What many Americans fail to realize is that retired politicians still maintain open lines of communication within the federal government, including sources within certain intelligence agencies. There are even times when sitting presidents call upon their predecessors for advice. Therefore, it was not surprising that the two friends were very well informed about the current dangers their nation faced.

Cal had interrupted the story to ask why any Democrat would even be caught dead with a former rival. He prefaced the question by pleading total ignorance about the political process and the players involved.

President Waller, the tallest of the group at around six foot five, chuckled and explained.

"You're not far off the mark, Cal. I won't lie to you. I was as liberal as they come when I first stepped into office. Funny thing about becoming President is that it humbled me. All of a sudden I was thrust into a whole new world. Yes, I had access to a lot before I was sworn in, but nothing prepared me for the reality."

Cal didn't understand. "What do you mean?"

"Let's just say it was like I'd been walking around with blinders on my whole life and then all of a sudden, they were gone."

Cal was beginning to understand. "So what changed for you?"

Waller laughed and spread his arms wide. "Everything. Now I was getting daily reports from our intelligence assets. I really began to think the intel guys were just trying to spook me, no pun intended. It seemed like every brief I got was about some communist faction or terrorist cell trying to wipe us off the planet. I suddenly realized how naïve I'd been."

"I'm confused, Mr. President. You took office back in the nineties. You just said the Council didn't form until after 9/11."

President Waller nodded, "First off, in this room we all go by our first names. We're all putting our necks on the line, including you. So start out by calling me Hank."

Cal was clearly uncomfortable by the request, but conceded, "OK, Hank."

"That's better. Now to answer your question. As a lot of my liberal predecessors have done, I moved away from the far Left toward the Center during my tenure. I couldn't make drastic changes overnight. People would think I was crazy AND I'd lose my electoral base. Hell, I'm not vain when I say I wanted to get reelected."

"So what else changed during your presidency?"

"I started listening."

"To who?"

Waller motioned to the entire group. "Everyone. It's a sad fact in the political arena that once you get a taste of power, you feel like you know everything. Now I wasn't totally close-minded, but I sure had an ego. I can tell you that now without being embarrassed. So I started listening to the experts, namely the operators in intelligence and the military. I really had no idea how smart some of you guys are."

President Kelton motioned to his colleague. "Let me chime in for a second, Hank."

Waller grabbed his drink and toasted his friend. "Have at it, Johnny."

Kelton toasted back, "I just wanted to tell Cal that our red-headed Democratic stepchild was not the only one to experience a wakeup call. I think if you ask each man in this room, he'll tell you about some event that opened his eyes to the threats confronting America."

Waller nodded and replied, "That's right. And I guess that's the point. The nine men you see here today experienced an awakening. First and foremost, we are all American patriots. We believe our nation is the greatest in the world. We are a beacon of hope for so many. We are also a perfect target."

"So you guys came out of retirement?"

Kelton answered, "I don't think politicians ever retire. We just move on to other things. You know, fundraising, support, opening libraries, consulting..."

"I'm assuming you don't publicize this group."

Waller shifted in his seat. "That's right. Could you imagine what would happen if the media found out that a bunch of retired politicians are working to save America? They'd either think we were a higher form of radical militia or just put us in jail. No, we won't ever be going public."

Kelton looked back to Cal, "Cal, we all take this risk willingly. We know that we can't just stand back and do nothing. I'm thinking that you would understand that more than most."

Cal nodded and thought about his recent out-of-bounds operation to take down the gang leader, Dante West, who killed Cal's fiancé the year before. Did these men know what he'd done?

Cal nodded seriously. "Okay. So tell me how I fit in."

"Well, Travis tells us that you're about to take over the reins with us," said Waller.

"I'm still not entirely sure what that entails," Cal shrugged.

"Obviously, we don't get together much, what with our Secret Service entourage and all. We usually have to come up with some excuse. This go-around, we're accepting Travis's invite for some hunting in the area. It's not the easiest thing to cart us around. But from time to time, we come upon certain intelligence that has to be exploited outside the normal channels. SSI has become one of the tools we use to go operational."

"So how did you guys find us?" Cal asked.

Waller took a sip of his drink. "I met your dad back in the nineties when I was in office. Didn't know him well at the time. SSI handled some of my personal security just after 9/11 too. The Secret Service was stretched so thin that they had to augment with outside personnel. Travis came down with the crew he'd assigned to me. We hit it off after he found out I liked duck hunting and football. When Johnny and I came up with the idea for this group Travis was the first person I contacted."

"But why SSI? Why not go through your old government contacts?" Cal prodded.

Waller answered with a shrug, "We tried. Believe me we tried. Problem was that in the aftermath of 9/11, all of our agencies were overwhelmed. We had to find another ally."

"So you guys met with Travis and then what?"

"He agreed to take a look at what we found. It took a couple times to work out the kinks, but we've got a better system now," answered Waller.

Travis, who'd kept quiet, finally entered the conversation. "Normally we communicate over a secure network Neil developed. The Council will send over the intel they want analyzed. We do some digging and give them our answer."

The look of incredulity gave away Cal's next question. "I may be stating the obvious, but this feels way off the reservation."

Waller lost all the humor and his eyes and responded seriously. "It is. Just like your Corps Justice."

Cal's eyes went cold for a split second. He'd have to remember that these were men of power. They were used to knowing everything. They knew about his completely illegal operation to take down Dante West. *Calm down, Cal. You should've been prepared for that.*

Waller nodded and continued, "Yes, we know about your dad's credo. That's actually what convinced us to go with SSI."

President Waller reached into his pocket and pulled out what looked like a business card. Cal knew what it was. He had an identical, if somewhat worn, version of the same card. It was the *Corps Justice* card his father had given him before his death. Cal took the ex-President's card and read it for maybe the thousandth time.

<u>CORPS JUSTICE</u>
1. WE WILL PROTECT AND DEFEND THE CONSTITUTION OF THE UNITED STATES.
2. WE WILL PROTECT THE WEAK AND PUNISH THE WICKED.
3. WHEN THE LAWS OF THIS NATION HINDER THE COMPLETION OF THESE DUTIES, OUR MORAL COMPASS WILL GUIDE US TO SEE THE MISSION THROUGH.

Cal wondered quietly whether this was what his father had in mind. Taking out a ruthless criminal was one thing; doing the dirty work for a bunch of politicians was another story.

"I know what you're thinking, Cal. Never trust a politician, right?" Waller asked innocently.

The bluntness surprised Cal. "I...I don't mean to be disrespectful, but...yes."

Waller laughed. "We're gonna get along just fine. Sounds like a chip off the old block, Trav."

"He is," smirked Travis.

"Did your dad ever tell you the story about meeting me?" President Waller asked.

Cal shook his head. "I don't think so."

"Let me give you the abridged version. I think I mentioned earlier that we'd met during my presidency. Some of my top military aides had recommended calling in your dad for more intel on the Middle East. Saddam was being a real pain in the ass and SSI had assets all over Iraq. So your dad shows up and answers all of our questions. Then one of my more enthusiastic junior aides starts grilling your dad on the legality of how the information was obtained. I didn't really approve, but I let the conversation run its course. I wanted to see how your dad would handle it."

Travis chuckled, "You'll love this, Cal."

"He's right. Long story short, your dad proceeds to calmly dissect this young aide's political career, along with a few non-discreet details about his dirty private life. Your dad made it pretty plain that he hated politicians and completely embarrassed his accuser. I think the only reason he showed up that day was because he thought it was his patriotic duty."

"That sounds like dad," answered Cal with a chuckle of his own.

Waller continued, "I walked away from that incident with two thoughts: one, that your dad was a Marine through and through; and two, that I never wanted to be on his bad side."

Travis interrupted, "I've known these gentlemen for a while now, Cal. I wanted you to meet them today so you could see with your own eyes. They are not typical politicos. They're American patriots just like us."

Waller suddenly stood and pointed at the American flag in the corner. "Damn right, and we're gonna do anything we can to keep this country safe."

✝ ✝ ✝

There was a part of Cal that still couldn't come to grips with his new life. If he could tell anyone what he did for a living, they'd never believe it.

Cal finished up his shower and dried off. It was time to get back to work.

Chapter 3
Washington, D.C.
10:40am, September 13th

CONGRESSMAN BRANDON ZIMMER was in no mood to talk. After a lot of soul-searching, he'd decided to tell his father about the incident in Las Vegas. He waited for the senior Senator to make the walk from his senate chambers. He'd instructed his small staff to take an extended lunch break. Father and son would have the office alone. Brandon tapped his foot nervously as he waited.

Senator Zimmer strolled into Brandon's office precisely ten minutes after their phone conversation. The elder statesman was the very picture of a political figure. Completely gray haired, his frame was still fit from vigorous daily exercise. He'd competed in triathlons in his younger days, but now whetted his competitive appetite on the tennis courts, typically throttling his peers. Senator Zimmer was a card-carrying Democrat, but was well respected on both sides of the aisle. He'd mellowed with age but his temper was still legendary.

Senator Zimmer cut to the chase. "So what is it this time, Brandon?"

Brandon tried to look his father in the face as he answered, "I've got a problem."

The Senator rolled his eyes. "What else is new?"

The young Congressman pounded his fist on the side table. "Dad, this time it's really serious."

Brandon knew better than to lie to his father, so he quickly ran through the details of Beth's murder in Las Vegas. Senator Zimmer stayed quiet during the most of the recitation. He only interrupted his son twice to clarify points.

As Brandon wrapped up his tale, Sen. Zimmer walked to the Congressman's large desk and sat down. He placed his hands on the desk and glared at his only son.

"Well Brandon, I'd love to know how you're going to get your tail out of this one."

Chapter 4
Las Vegas, Nevada
11:30am, September 13th

THE SMALL GROUP OF MEN sat quietly in the windowless gloom of the hotel conference room. Smoke from carefully tended cigarettes curled towards the ceiling and hovered. They all knew each other. Theirs was a relationship kindled over years of collaboration. No man was younger than fifty-five.

They'd gathered as friends but considered each other family. In fact, some had betrothed their children to the offspring of fellow members.

Every head around the table digested the latest reports from their appointed leader. The time for decisive action was coming. The Empire of Japan would rise again.

Chapter 5
Turks and Caicos, Providenciales Island
12:02pm, September 13th

CAL ADJUSTED THE REMOTE CAMERA. After only an hour on surveillance, he was bored. The only way he could keep focused was to continuously pan and zoom the view. Not that he could complain though. He'd volunteered for the gig against Travis's objections.

As head of the newly dubbed Strategies and Contingencies Division (SCD) of SSI, Cal should have been at one of SSI's two headquarters, one south of Nashville and one outside of Charlottesville, Virginia.

Travis, Cal's cousin and CEO of SSI, wanted Cal to coordinate his division's future plans.

Despite the conveniently unhelpful name given to SSI's newest branch, it was in fact the covert wing of the Stokes Security International. Unknown to the public and government agencies, at times SSI worked outside the law. Through its contacts, like the Council of Patriots, SSI gathered actionable intelligence that would otherwise go unused by law enforcement and even the most covert of government agencies. The reasons were twofold: first, the intelligence itself could never be used in a court of law because of the methods by which it was obtained and second, the secret division was only tasked with threats to the American homeland.

SSI's special operations brethren could take care of the international threats. Politicians were loath to deploy troops on American soil. That left agencies like the FBI, Homeland Security and local law enforcement to the task. Those agencies are still bound by law to employ due process and not infringe on individual liberties. The Patriot Act helped, but not in all cases.

It was Cal's father who had decided to help the cause. Instead of standing by, watching helplessly as America was devoured from both the outside and within, Cal Sr. decided to act. Employing his mantra of *Corps Justice*, he took his covert battle to the enemy.

Targets over the previous years included drug lords, terrorists, mass murderers, and more. The common thread? Each target knew enough about American law to skirt law enforcement. Technology had allowed the enemies of the United States to further entrench themselves into North America.

Cal Sr. realized the immense danger this would create for his corporation. He'd therefore carefully picked those involved for their sense of integrity, patriotism, and ability to choose right from wrong. It didn't hurt that one and all were former warriors from their respective branches of the Armed Forces.

Years later, it was Cal, Jr. who'd been tapped to exact this covert justice. It was a thankless job, but each man involved was used to serving his country and barely getting a pat on the back. To a man, the most important aspect was protecting America from growing internal threats. There was no sleep lost for their slain enemies. There was only the dream of a brighter future and a more secure America.

He was currently in Turks and Caicos with a small SSI surveillance team. Nothing fancy, just a week of staring at a camera and following a high profile target around the small Caribbean island. Since taking over the new division Cal had made it a point to get a feel for all operational aspects at SSI. He'd spent time with the insertion teams, the security teams, an unfortunate weekend with the VIP protection teams (Cal couldn't stand kissing up to snobby elite), the Research and Development Division headed up by his good friend Neil Patel, and finally the surveillance teams. Cal had also been through a majority of the training programs provided by his company, such as the close quarters combat training and the hand-to-hand training led by

MSgt Willy Trent. He still had a green bruise from their last training session on the mats.

It had taken him away from the strategic planning Travis had wanted, but in the long run it gave Cal a better understanding of SSI's capabilities. As a Marine, he had to be familiar with all the parts of an operational unit. It also allowed him to be on the ground with the troops. It was one of the things he still missed about being in the Marine Corps.

He'd always known that SSI made a lot of money, but he never knew exactly where it came from. In its infancy, the bulk of the company's work came from security, training, and surveillance contracts. SSI still had a large contract force in Iraq and Afghanistan.

They'd slowly moved away from operational work and branched into cyber warfare and R&D. Not only did SSI provide equipment and weapons systems for the United States government, it also developed software and products for civilian corporations. With Neil in the lead, SSI had grown into a virtual factory of American commerce.

Cal was proud of the fact that his company now quietly led many of the most innovative brands in the world. Neil had even created a technology incubator that annually selected twenty technology start-ups from around the world, provided them with $100,000 for one year, mentored them through the rigors of launching, and allowed them to work in close proximity with either the Nashville or Charlottesville headquarters of SSI. The company would, of course, retain twenty percent of each venture.

Over the past three years, out of the sixty start-ups they'd sponsored, thirty-two were already profitable. Six had already been sold to the likes of Google, Apple, and GE to the tune of 150 million dollars.

Cal's mind wandered as he stared at the high-def screen. This stint had been more of a vacation than an undercover operation. The big fat target they were getting paid to monitor did little more than eat, sit by the pool, and sleep. Even his entourage rarely left the confines of the beautiful resort.

His cell phone buzzed silently in his pocket as Cal struggled to stay awake. He pulled it out of his shorts, looked at the caller ID and answered.

It was his cousin. "Hey, Trav."

"I heard a nasty rumor that Willy drank you under the table, cuz."

Cal laughed. "Ain't no rumor, Trav. I woke a sleeping giant and lost."

"I could've told you that would happen!" Travis laughed back.

"I know. You live and learn."

Suddenly serious, Travis asked, "Hey, something just came up. How quickly can you get back here?"

"Are you in Tennessee or Virginia?"

"Virginia."

"I guess I could catch a flight tomorrow. We only have two more days left on this gig anyway."

"I need you back sooner."

Cal was curious about the sudden urgency. "You wanna give me a hint of what's going on?"

"We've had a request from the Council and they're bringing an outsider to come see us."

An outsider? Cal couldn't think of who it might be. "Huh. Let me make a couple calls and see if I can't get out tonight."

"Call me when you know," Travis said and finished the call.

Cal replaced his phone and looked back up at the screen. The obese target was still lying in bed rubbing his rotund belly. Maybe it was time to go.

Chapter 6
Camp Cavalier, Charlottesville, VA
7:45am, September 14th

CAL WALKED INTO the Headquarters building of SSI's Charlottesville outpost, Camp Cavalier. He tiredly nodded to the guard at the front desk. Sporting a three-day beard and the remnants of a red-eye flight gone wrong (they'd hit foul weather upon take-off and landing), Cal was quite a sight.

The guard chuckled as he glanced up at Cal. "Good trip back?"

Cal smiled with a sigh. "You better watch what you say or I may walk close enough that you can smell me."

The guard put up his hands and shook his head. "No thanks. Can I help you with your gear?"

"I'm good. I'll just make a quick run down to the showers and get cleaned up."

The guard looked a little embarrassed to add, "Travis asked that you come to his office as soon as you got here."

"I'll tell him you told me, but I'll be damned if I'll walk in there smelling the way I do."

The guard shook his head again and waved, "Good luck, Cal."

Cal made his way to the staff locker room and took a much-needed shower. Ten minutes later he emerged wearing a slightly mussed pair of cargo shorts and collared shirt. It was the best he'd managed from his assorted island wear. There hadn't been time to stop and get anything nicer.

Oh well. They'd have to deal with it. Cal wasn't much for fancy appearances these days anyway.

He walked by Travis's secretary who looked at Cal with an arched eyebrow. Cal ignored the look with a nod and knocked on Travis's door.

"Come in," Travis barked from inside.

Cal walked into the large office and glanced at the sitting area. Travis was seated, facing two men dressed in impeccable suits. They looked vaguely familiar and had similar bone structure. *Father and son?* Cal thought.

"Cal, I'd like to introduce you to Senator Zimmer and Congressman Zimmer." Travis stood as he motioned toward his guests.

Cal shook both men's hands and took a seat next to Travis. The younger Zimmer seemed to be sizing him up almost disgustedly. Cal didn't like the vibe he was getting from Junior.

"Gentlemen, I'd like to apologize for my appearance. I hopped on the first flight I could bribe myself onto."

"Not to worry, Cal. We just appreciate you getting here so quickly," Senator Zimmer responded kindly.

Travis continued, "Cal, this meeting was arranged by some mutual friends. The Senator has a slightly sticky situation he'd like our help with."

Cal knew that "mutual friends" meant the Council of Patriots. No doubt the elder Senator knew one or more members. It was strange to be meeting with current members of the U.S. government. Cal couldn't wait to hear what this was all about.

"How can I help, Senator?" Cal asked.

"As Travis said, a mutual friend suggested I call you about a little problem my son has," the Senator answered cryptically.

"Little problem?"

"I believe my son is being framed, Mr. Stokes," Zimmer answered, suddenly serious.

Cal looked over at the younger politician then back to Senator Zimmer. "In what way?"

Senator Zimmer proceeded to tell the entire sordid tale. Cal simply sat in stunned silence. Congressman Zimmer looked like a beaten dog, eyes cast to the floor.

Cal finally answered, "I'm sorry, Senator, but I don't quite understand why you need our help. Wouldn't the Secret Service or FBI be a better fit?"

Senator Zimmer shook his head almost sadly. "Unfortunately, no. As much as I would love to see my son learn the lesson on his own, an episode of this caliber would not only destroy my son, but would also send untold ripples through Washington."

"I don't mean to repeat myself, Senator, but I'm still confused about what you want us to do."

"Find out who's doing this to my son."

Cal looked to Travis for guidance. He was in completely uncharted territory on this one. A murdered woman. A seemingly guilty Congressman. A famous Senator. What the hell was HE supposed to do? Never one to take the easy approach, Cal pressed on.

"It seems to me that if Congressman Zimmer would resign and turn himself in, all this would be a moot point."

Brandon Zimmer jumped out his chair and pointed at Cal. "Oh, you'd like that wouldn't you! I don't have to sit here and listen..."

"Shut up and sit down, Brandon! I'm sorry, Mr. Stokes. Apparently my son still doesn't appreciate the gravity of the situation."

Cal nodded skeptically. If they wanted the truth, he'd give it to them. It looked like Junior was about to have a nervous breakdown.

Cal continued, "Senator, let's say we do end up helping you, what do you want us to do once we've determined who the guilty party is?"

"I'm not asking you to do anything you're not comfortable with. What if we just start with finding out who they are. Once we have that, we can make a decision on which way to turn."

Cal thought for a minute. It didn't sound like anything too overt. Maybe it'd end up being a little surveillance. The one thing Cal wasn't looking forward to was dealing with Congressman Zimmer.

"I'll do it on one condition, Senator."

Sen. Zimmer's eyebrow rose. "And what would that be, Mr. Stokes?"

"Your son has to do EXACTLY what I say."

Over the strong objections of his son, Sen. Richard Zimmer answered with a wry smile, "Done."

Chapter 7
Camp Cavalier, Charlottesville, VA
8:39am, September 14th

"**YOU COULD'VE GIVEN ME** a heads-up, Trav." Cal frowned at his cousin. The last thing he wanted to do was babysit a spoiled politician.

Travis smiled. "If I'd told you who it was and what they wanted, you would've figured out some way not to make it back. This way we both win."

"How do I win?"

"You get your first action with the Council. It's great that I've vouched for you, but until you prove yourself, they won't know what to do with us."

"But I thought we were in tight with these guys."

Travis walked over to his desk as he explained. "We've had contact with the Council off and on for last few years. The problem is that we never had anyone dedicated to utilizing their intel. I was their contact, but I also had to run SSI. It pulled me thin. Now that we've got you, we can put some muscle behind it."

"So what's my guidance going forward?"

"I'm not gonna hold your hand or look over your shoulder, Cal. In this case, I want to push you. Take a look at the file we've started compiling. I think you'll find some interesting tidbits about the Vegas underground. Plus, I completely agree with the Senator. Despite Congressman Zimmer's past, the whole bloody murder scenario isn't his M.O. He's being set up for something."

Cal realized he'd allowed his emotions to cloud his objectivity. Maybe Travis was right. Maybe there was something to the story.

"Okay. I'll handle it."

"Alright. Why don't you head down to Intel and see if you can't dig up anything else. In the meantime, come up with a team and a plan. Let me know if you need something special."

Cal walked out of Travis's office and headed to his personal cubicle. They'd offered him his father's office but he'd declined. The old man's office was more of a shrine now. Besides, Cal enjoyed the thought of working his way up the ladder and being with his troops.

The first thing he needed to do was pick his A-team. Then it was off to Sin City.

Chapter 8
Las Vegas, Nevada
2:48am, September 16th

THE WORKMEN LOADED the large packages into the nearly full semis. They were all getting paid hefty overtime for working through the night. It was almost three in the morning but the boxes weren't particularly heavy. There were just a lot of them. The only pain for the crew was dealing with the quiet little Japanese guy and his big Russian friend.

The smaller Asian man was obviously in charge. He gave clipped orders and maintained an intense vigil over the loading process. The large Russian looked bored as he gazed lazily around the small truck terminal. He hadn't made a sound except for the occasionally spit of phlegm over the metal railing.

"Hey boss, how much longer we got?"

Max Unger looked back at his worker. "Until we get all these trailers loaded, shithead. Now shut up and go back to work."

The worker grumbled and headed back to the smallest stack of packages. Max stole a look at the man who'd offered a tidy sum if the shipment could be processed in one night. Unger had almost refused, but the enticement of so much cash won him over. Even as he was anticipating his payday, Max Unger couldn't shake the feeling of unease as he loaded yet another stamped cardboard box. *What the hell is in these boxes?*

Chapter 9
Camp Spartan, Arrington, Tennessee
7:37am, September 16th

IT TOOK CAL TWO DAYS to piece together an initial plan of attack and gather his team. He'd recalled Neil Patel and MSgt Trent from Turks. The other members of the advance team included his good friend and former Navy Corpsman Brian Ramirez. Brian was currently heading-up the battle-med research team inside Patel's R&D department. SSI focused heavily on new development not only to make money, but also to better support American troops serving around the globe.

Cal figured that the first thing to do was take a look around Vegas and see what cropped up. Dumb luck just might expose Zimmer's enemies without much effort.

The small team chatted quietly as Cal gathered his notes. He finally looked up. "You guys have a good trip back?"

"First Class is always nice when I'm not the one paying for it," Willy joked in his booming voice.

"Top told me all about your little competition at the tiki bar, Cal," Brian interrupted grinning. "I knew you were a dumb grunt, but waking the sleeping giant..."

Cal raised his hands in defeat. "I know, I know. I'll never live that one down. Let me run you through what we've got."

Cal recounted the Congressman's story. He also outlined Zimmer's past and what he'd been able to dig up about Ishi Nakamura, which wasn't much. Eyebrows were raised, but they waited for Cal to finish before asking questions.

"So the first thing we need to do is link Top up with Congressman Zimmer. You'll be tapped as his new bodyguard. We've already floated the story of some weirdo sending Zimmer some threatening letters. Now, Top, this guy might end up being a royal pain in the ass, but I need you to stick close to him," Cal instructed. "Neil, I'll need you to be around for technical support. Bring anything you think you might need. Brian and I will be posing as tourists. We'll take in the sights and do a little gambling. I want to see if we can weed out anyone following Zimmer. Any questions?"

Brian spoke up first. "Why only four of us? Don't you think we might need some more manpower?"

Cal shook his head. "This is just our initial reconnaissance. I don't want whoever's framing Zimmer to know we're there. The smaller the team, the less likely it'll be that we get spotted."

"You want me to do some more background on this Ishi guy?" Neil asked.

"Yeah. I couldn't find much. Seemed pretty normal on paper. His parents came over from Japan when he was a kid. Grew up in San Francisco. Did well in school. Met Zimmer at Harvard. A few jobs and internships here and there. Typical post-college stuff. I really want to know more about this company he works for."

"I'll get on it," Neil answered as he turned his attention to the mini-laptop perched on his knees.

Cal knew that if anybody could penetrate an organization with technology, it was Neil Patel. The certified genius wasn't just a whiz with gadgets, he was also a world-class hacker.

"Top, we'll fly you out to D.C. tomorrow. You can link up with the Congressman and then fly out to Vegas with him. Anything else?"

No one had anything to add. Everyone was already mentally coming up with their own game plan for the operation. Cal knew better than to get in their way. They were all proven operators. Even Neil was a warrior in his own way. All they needed was a quick snapshot. The rest would evolve once they got to Las Vegas.

Chapter 10
Las Vegas, Nevada
7:52am, September 16th

"WHAT IS THE STATUS of the shipment?"

"The packages are ready and each truck is awaiting my order to depart."

"Do you expect the packages to be delivered by the time we requested?"

"Yes. We have allowed extra time in case of weather or some other unforeseen circumstance."

"Good. Then you may proceed with the delivery."

The older man's assistant bowed respectfully and exited the palatial suite. The master took another drag from his cigarette and gazed out at the desert landscape.

Soon America would feel the pain and humiliation he'd long planned.

Chapter 11
Falls Church, VA
1:46pm, September 16th

MSGT WILLY TRENT STEPPED out of the taxi and paid the driver. It'd been an easy ride over from Reagan National. It still amazed him how close the nation's capital looked as you landed. You could see everything.

Unfortunately, this wouldn't be a tourist stop. His orders were clear: keep eyes-on Congressman Brandon Zimmer, 24/7.

He strolled up to the modest home and quickly scanned the finely manicured lawn. Access to the property looked easy. No obvious security. Strange. He'd have to change that.

Trent knocked and waited patiently for the door to open. He was surprised when Congressman Zimmer opened the door. *No interior security either?*

The good-looking congressman smiled and reached out his hand. "You must be Master Sergeant Trent."

"Yes, sir. Although most people call me Willy or Top."

"Top's the nickname you Marines call Master Sergeants, right?" Zimmer asked still smiling congenially.

"Only the ones they like, sir," Trent smiled back.

"Well, come on in. I'll give you a quick tour of the place and then you can fill me in on your team's plan." Zimmer ushered Willy in through the door and led the way to the back of the house, highlighting the layout as they went. The hallway opened up to a large great room that overlooked Lake Barcroft. Trent could see a couple families enjoying the early fall weather on their pontoon boats. He wondered quietly whether there was any security on the sprawling back lawn either.

"Can I get you anything, Top?"

"No thank you, sir. Maybe we should go over your itinerary."

Zimmer's smile slipped for a split-second, but was replaced quickly. Trent noticed. *Obviously this guy isn't used to being on someone else's schedule.*

"Why not? Tell me what you guys have come up with." Zimmer walked over to the closest armchair and took a seat.

Maybe this guy ain't as bad as Cal thinks. We'll see.

"First, sir, my orders are pretty clear. I'm supposed to be with you 24/7. No exceptions."

To Zimmer's credit, not even the faintest hint of anger crossed his face. "I understand, Top. I assume you already know the whole story?"

Trent nodded.

"Then you know I'm not really in a position to fight this. You guys are doing me a favor and I really do appreciate it. Democrat or not, I'm no idiot."

"No disrespect intended, sir. I've just always found that it's better to the clear the air and manage expectations in the beginning."

Willy looked to Zimmer for questions but none came. "So to start I wanted to ask you some questions about your property here."

Trent grilled Zimmer for close to an hour. He quickly found that the security in the rented residence was decent but still lacking, despite the Las Vegas episode. The only things in place were a monitoring system supplied by a local vendor and a panic number provided to all incoming members of the House of Representatives.

It was clearly evident that the freshman representative was somewhat naïve about personal protection and surveillance. It wasn't unusual for unknown Congressmen to drive their own cars, but

Willy got the distinct feeling that prior to the Vegas incident, Zimmer almost felt untouchable. Zimmer explained that he'd clearly been instructed by Ishi not to increase any security after the girl's murder. Brandon wasn't stupid. He knew the lack of security meant easy access for his blackmailers.

"Have you noticed anyone following you, anything strange?"

"Are you kidding? I see shadows everywhere now. I'd started to think I was really losing my grip on reality," Zimmer answered in a tone colored with panic.

"That's why I'm here, Congressman. I'll need to do some upgrades to your system here, but we'll do that through SSI, so whoever's watching you won't know. The next part of the plan is to take a little trip to Vegas. Cal wants to see if we can't get these rats out of their nest."

Brandon didn't want to go anywhere near Las Vegas. "No way! The minute I step into that place they'll be all over me. They've already had me back for a couple of mandatory meetings. Every time I feel like I'm the fish in the fishbowl. I'm surrounded and subtlety reminded of where I stand. I can't handle it!"

Willy shouldn't have been surprised by the outburst, but he was. He'd have to tread carefully on this one.

"Sir, as long as I'm with you, nothing will happen. Besides, we'll keep the visit as public as we can."

Zimmer wouldn't be mollified. "They'll see right through it. Why would I want to go out there anyway?"

"Cal's cooked up a story that we're floating out to the media. We've got contacts with prominent casino owners who are big political donors. One of them has a local job placement charity for disabled vets. He'd love for you to come out and help publicize it."

"What!? Those guys are all Republicans! I'll look like an idiot! I need to call my father on this before..."

"Sir, Senator Zimmer already knows."

"There's no way he'd approve this. I'll be a pariah!"

"Maybe you should look at it in a different way, sir. This group is all about job creation, helping military veterans and the local economy. You'd be doing a good thing."

"Cal's just trying to piss me off, isn't he?" Zimmer said dejectedly.

"I won't say that, sir, but maybe it'll be good for you. Besides, if you don't mind me saying, your political career isn't exactly shooting the moon right now."

Zimmer stared at his huge new bodyguard. The last thing he expected was a mountain with brains to show up on his doorstep. He'd assumed that Cal would send some dumb muscle-head to babysit him. At least he'd have someone to talk to now.

"You're right. When do we leave?"

Chapter 12
En-route to Las Vegas, Nevada
1:29pm, September 16th

CAL TOOK THE CRANBERRY juice from the stewardess. "Thanks."

The pretty blonde looked down at him. "Not a problem, sir. Please let me know if you need anything else." Her gaze lingered for a second and then she moved on to serve other passengers.

"I think she likes you, brother," Brian Ramirez teased from beside Cal.

"Not my type, Doc."

"You haven't had a type for a long time, Cal. What happened to that girl you met at the conference we went to?"

"Who?"

"You know. The one with the nice ass. Sabrina?"

"Oh, Salina. She was alright. The long distance thing wasn't for me."

Cal took a sip of his juice. Would he ever be ready? He wasn't conceited; he knew he was good looking. Above average height, still boyish but with the build of a man. He just couldn't get Jess out of his head. She'd been the one. The one that stopped his heart for the first time. Now she was at eternal rest overlooking Camp Spartan.

Brian looked at his friend and read his thoughts. "Not ready are you?"

Cal shook his head. "Not even close. Every time I talk to a girl I feel like I'm cheating."

"That's natural, man. Forget I even mentioned it. So like I was saying before, where do you want to hit first?" The look of excitement on Brian's face almost made Cal spit out his cranberry juice. He looked like a kid going to Disney World for the first time.

"How is it that you've never been to Vegas before?"

"Never had the chance. Left home at eighteen for the Navy, saw the world, then ended up back in Nashville."

Cal didn't want to spoil it for his friend. Las Vegas had some great stuff to see and eat, but he could never shake the contrast of wealth and poverty every time he visited. Vegas was littered with lost souls seeking an instant fortune or last drink. It wasn't all bad. The city was doing some great things for the arts and large corporations. Zappos had recently relocated to the area.

"You know, we do have to do some work while we're there," Cal replied almost seriously.

Brian shook his head. "You said this was a recon mission. That'll leave plenty of time to get fat and happy. I've been reading all about the buffet at the Bellagio. Did you know that they have all you can eat lobster?! I'm gonna eat 'til I fall over."

Cal chuckled. "Alright, Doc. Haven't they let you out of the Bat Cave? You sound like you've been sequestered for the past month."

"We've just been really busy. I'm trying to get these new Robo-Tourniquets to MARSOC."

"Robo-Tourniquets?" Cal asked.

"Yeah! It's fucking brilliant. One of the problems we've had on the battlefield was proper ways of maintaining pressure on injured arms or legs. The tourniquets in med kits have gotten better, but you've still got guys pulling off bootlaces and shredding their utilities to tie-off wounds. A lot of times, by the time the evac gets to a field hospital, the limb can't be saved. We always knew that there was a pressure threshold to decrease blood loss while maintaining good blood flow. The problem is you can't always manually monitor that when you're getting shot at. That's why we built the Robo-Tourniquet."

"I think you lost me, Doc." Cal knew all about the project from Neil, but wanted to hear it from Brian. It was the first R&D invention the former corpsman had spearheaded himself.

"So you've seen those blood pressure cuffs you can buy at the store, right?"

Cal nodded.

"Basically, we started out with one of those. Neil helped me rig one so we could actually program in the optimum pressure for a given wound and body type, then the cuff does it automatically. We've tested it with my paramedic buddies at Vanderbilt and they love it. It takes away the guessing game and lets a total amateur save someone's life and limb."

Cal was truly happy for his friend. They'd met just over a year before. Cal the patient, Brian the nurse. Ramirez was there when Cal needed a friend most after the loss of his fiancé. Brian's faith in Cal turned into a strong friendship. He thought it was always funny how former military guys tended to bond if the initial introductions went well. Somehow they were able to skip a few levels of trust, bypass the B.S. and become buds.

After the episode with the gangster, Dante West, Brian was offered a full-time position at SSI. It wasn't a hard decision for him. Although he loved his job at Vandy, he still missed the camaraderie of the Navy and Marine Corps. SSI provided not only a challenge, but the brotherhood so many military vets long for after separating from the service.

Brian fit in easily with the team at SSI. Athletic like the rest, his easy-going attitude endeared him to even the most hardcore of SSI operators. It didn't hurt that Brian was also a Silver Star recipient for saving the lives of his fellow warriors in Iraq.

"Anything else you want to do in Vegas?" Cal asked.

"I heard about a few new clubs that could be fun. Maybe I can practice some of those counter-surveillance techniques Dunn's been teaching me."

Todd Dunn was head of internal security at Stokes Security International. Dunn was also a former Ranger that rarely broke from his serious demeanor.

"Have you ever seen that dude disappear in a crowd? It's unbelievable!"

Cal knew most people underestimated the burly Dunn. What strangers never knew was the cunning and brilliance inside the soldier's mind. He looked like a typical meat-head but could easily run with the best tacticians in the game. Dunn wasn't a bad chess player either. He'd trounced Cal on more than one occasion.

"Yeah. I remember when I went through his Urban Escape and Evade course earlier this year. He took a couple of us to the Green Hills Mall. The place wasn't even close to being packed and we lost him in under a minute. Later he shows up with a detailed description of what I'd done for the whole time. Guy knows his stuff," affirmed Cal.

The stewardess appeared and asked if she could get the companions anything before landing.

"I think we're good..." Cal paused to remember the girl's name.

"Veronica," she replied with a dazzling smile.

"Veronica," Cal repeated, "thanks for everything."

She disappeared down the aisle and Brian took the opportunity to lean over Cal and get a last peek of Veronica's exit.

"You sure you're not ready yet?" Brian asked his friend.

Chapter 13
Washington, D.C.
2:10pm, September 16th

"IS EVERYTHING IN position?" the career politician asked into the secure phone.

"Yes. All teams are standing by for your authorization."

"Good. As we discussed, once I give you the go-ahead the operation must commence within twenty-four hours."

"Understood."

"I won't have any problems with your compatriots will I?"

"No. As long as you hold up your end of the bargain, you will soon be the next President of the United States."

The politician sat back and smiled. He'd waited a long time for this opportunity. He couldn't wait to show that moron in the Oval Office what a real leader looked like. "We've known each other a long time. Have I ever gone back on my word?"

The man on the other end paused. "We only wish to ensure all parties will move forward together. Once again, our nations will be allied on the same path."

The politician honestly didn't give a damn for his partner's motives. This was all about securing the American presidency.

"You provide what we agreed on and your little empire will rise again," he sneered into the phone.

"It will be done."

The politician replaced the receiver. The Democratic National Convention was right around the corner. This one would be absolutely historic. The nation and his party would soon be desperate for a new leader. *I'll be damned if I'll wait another four years.* Maybe it was time to write his acceptance speech.

Chapter 14
Las Vegas, Nevada
3:16pm, September 16th

CAL AND BRIAN CHECKED into their room at the Cosmopolitan Hotel and Casino. It was located in an ideal location at the end of The Strip. Close enough to Neil at the Bellagio, it was also within easy walking distance to Congressman Zimmer at Zeitaku just off The Strip.

Cal glanced at his watch. "Top and Zimmer should be flying in soon. Let's head over to the Bellagio and check out what Neil's got."

Although it was only early afternoon, Las Vegas Boulevard was already packed with tourists. The pair made their way through the throngs and finally arrived at the Bellagio.

"Wow! This place is crazy!" Brian exclaimed.

"You talking about all the people or the hotel?"

"Both! Is it always like this?"

Cal kept reminding himself not to dampen the mood. Brian needed to enjoy the experience.

"The hotel looks even more beautiful at night. We'll come check it out later. As for the people, I guess the cooler weather's really brought out the masses this year."

"Does it have anything to do with the convention?" Brian asked.

"Which one? They have a ton out here."

"Do you ever watch the news, jarhead? The Democratic National Convention."

"I get all my news on Drudge, Doc. Besides, why the hell would I care about the left side of the aisle?"

"We are helping out a Democratic Congressman. You know what The Hammer says. Do..."

"Yeah, yeah. Do your homework." Cal interrupted impatiently. The Hammer was SSI's lead attorney Marjorie Haines. She'd picked up the nickname not only for her ferocity in the courtroom, but also the way she regularly took down SSI operators on the training mats. It was rumored that she had an impressive array of vintage wines aging in her cellar, thanks in part to the lucrative bets she'd won from SSI warriors. As the only female employee at SSI (a distinction she was silently proud of and didn't care to share), there was always a challenge especially from cocky newcomers.

The Hammer was also meticulous about preparation. She knew more about impending ops than most of the men going into the field. It was a habit she hammered into her peers constantly. Haines was a valued advisor to Travis (it was also rumored that the two had an on-again off-again romance on the side) and the rest of the SSI leadership team. Beautiful and deadly, she was a force to be reckoned with.

"So when is the convention?" Cal asked.

"This week."

The two walked in through the Bellagio's main entrance and headed for the elevators. Cal glanced around casually, further honing his counter surveillance skills. He knew that Las Vegas casinos were some of the most guarded fortresses on Earth. It would be interesting trying to pick out the enemies among the sea of native security staff.

They soon reached Patel's door and knocked on it.

Pointing to the small peephole Brian asked, "You think that's one of his rigged cameras?"

The tech genius was known for weaving surveillance gear into anything he could. It also made him one of the most successful pranksters on both SSI campuses.

"I'll bet it is," Cal answered. "What the hell's taking him so long?"

He knocked again. Nothing. Strange.

Cal pulled out his mobile and dialed Neil's number. Patel picked up on the third ring.

"Yeah?"

"Were you asleep?"

"Cal?"

"Yeah, jackass. We're right outside your door!"

"Oh, sorry. I'll be there in a sec."

Cal looked down at his phone and shook his head.

"He did get here yesterday, Cal. I'll bet he was out gambling all night," Brian said smirking.

The door opened and a bleary-eyed Neil peered out.

"Sorry guys. Pulled an all-nighter."

Brian beat Cal to the punch, "How much did you win?"

"What?" asked a clearly confused Patel as he stepped back into the room, Cal and Brian following.

"How much did you win at the craps tables last night?" Brian repeated.

"Oh! I wasn't gambling, Doc. I was getting all this set up." Patel motioned to the impressive array of equipment lining the room.

"Holy crap, Neil!" Cal piped, "Are you having an Xbox convention in here?"

"I wish. Figured we'd need as much horsepower as we could get. It was a real pain getting it shipped and setup yesterday. At least now I've got everything I'll need to work remotely." Neil scratched his disheveled hair and fixed his expensive eyeglasses. His handsome

Indian face was lined with two-day-old stubble. "You guys hungry?"

"We just grabbed a quick bite at our hotel," Cal explained. "You wanna order up some room service or give us a quick rundown of where we're at?"

Neil gave food a serious thought as he felt his stomach grumble. He knew better than to make his friend wait though. They'd know each other since their days at the University of Virginia, and Neil knew Cal could be an impatient and stubborn ass when he wanted to.

"Let me give you a brief summary and then I'll get some food."

Cal nodded and followed Neil over to the main bank of computer screens.

Patel sat down, logged in, and started clicking away on the mouse. Pictures popped up on multiple screens.

"Okay. Based on the information I got from Congressman Zimmer, I've started my analysis on this gaming consultancy: Ichiban Gaming. The only intel I've gathered on them is from their website and public records. I've got a couple of my crawler programs making some inquiries now." Neil pointed at the far left screen. "This guy right here is the Congressman's friend, Ishi Nakamura. Looked up his records and so far everything checks out. It does seem a little odd for him to be such a big fish at Ichiban at his age. Then again, it's his father's company so you never know."

Cal interrupted. "This guy is dirty, Neil. No way could he call off the hounds at a murder scene without having some pull. Do whatever you need to do to find out more."

"Already on it. I'm pulling his banking history right now. With that, I can track where he's been. Should know more soon."

"Okay. I'm going to Zimmer's hotel to take a look around. Do you have my order?" Cal asked.

"Yeah, it's all in that box." Neil pointed to a black case, about two feet by four feet in size, laying on the nearest chaise lounge.

Cal kneeled down and opened the case. Inside were three pistols and plenty of ammunition from the SSI armory. Nothing less than a .45. Cal ignored them. Walking into a Las Vegas hotel armed wasn't the best thing. Instead, he snagged one of four knives and pulled it out of the sheath. The blade, six inches in length, was pointed and razor sharp on both edges. He'd heard about these particular blades in one of his favorite novels and decided to order them a few months earlier. It was a small weapon but effective in a pinch. More importantly you could strap it to your wrist and carry it concealed. Retrieval was easy and deadly. After the attack in Nashville the previous year, Cal never left home unprepared. Although he would've loved his trusty Springfield XD pistol, the blade would do.

He looked up at Ramirez, pointing at the remaining weapons. "You want one?"

"I'm good. I'll stick with my pennies," Brian said, patting his jean pockets.

Brian was talking about the two sets of rolled pennies, one in each pocket. They weren't as good as a firearm, but very effective in a fistfight. Besides, Ramirez wasn't a stranger to hand-to-hand combat. He'd spent plenty of time in the Principal's office as a kid. Going to an all-white (save one) school in Nashville hadn't always been the easiest. There were always a couple of rednecks that wanted to pick on his Hispanic heritage. They soon found out that the little beaner was a scrapper, thanks to hours of practice in the boxing ring.

Cal took off his sport coat, strapped the knife onto his left arm, and put his coat back on. "You ready, Doc?"

"Let's go."

+ + +

"Father, the Congressman will be landing soon," Ishi bowed to his father.

Kazuo Nakamura, a slightly overweight man, looked at his son with pride. To think that all their plans were finally coming to fruition. Years of planning. Congressman Zimmer was the icing on the cake. Yes, delivered by their contact in Washington, but designed and executed by Ishi.

"Good. Ensure our eyes are always on him," he said as he stroked his graying goatee.

"Yes, Father. There has been one new development." Ishi offered cautiously.

"And what would that be, my Son?"

"It seems that the Congressman has a bodyguard with him."

"How did you find out about this?"

"Our contact sent me an encrypted email an hour ago. Apparently, the Congressman contacted a company called SSI to provide security."

"What?! The fool! You assured me that this would not happen."

"I warned him, Father. There is more."

All vestiges of Kazuo Nakamura's calm façade disappeared. "What else has he done?!"

"Our contact also alerted me to the fact that there might be additional SSI personnel coming to Las Vegas to conduct surveillance. He was only able to provide a brief profile of one man, a Calvin Stokes, Jr. Mr. Stokes is the heir to the company's founder; his deceased father."

Kazuo stroked his beard, thinking. "Did he provide a physical description?"

"He provided a picture from his military record. Calvin Stokes is a former Marine."

"Provide the photograph to the security staff at each of our hotels. If this Calvin Stokes sets foot in one of them I want him followed and apprehended...quietly."

"Should I use one of our teams?"

"No. Use our Russian friends. They know how to be discreet."

"Yes, Father. I will take care of it."

"Is there anything else?"

"No, Father."

"Our time is coming, my Son. Do well and our family will soon attain new heights within the empire."

Chapter 15
Las Vegas, Nevada
7:40pm, September 16th

DUSK WAS FALLING as the young man prepared. He splashed cold water on his face and looked into the bathroom mirror. His strong chiseled jaw was now covered with a shaggy beard. His blonde hair, once cut to military precision, hung to his shoulders. *I look more like a mountain man these days*, he thought. He finished in the bathroom and walked into the bedroom to collect his clothes and his weapons. Maybe tonight God would answer his call.

✚ ✚ ✚

Brian and Cal hadn't found anything of interest at the Congressman's hotel. There were some exclusive gambling rooms filled with foreign high-dollar players and two swanky Japanese restaurants, but nothing that stood out. At least now they had a better idea of the lay of the land.

Cal did not want to be in the hotel when Trent and the Congressman arrived. They'd already arranged a separate meeting outside of enemy territory for the next day.

The darkening sky found the duo walking the strip, meandering with the crowds. There wasn't any work to do tonight so they'd decided to see the sights.

"You want to hit that new club over by Caesar's? I think it's free before ten."

"Which one is that?" Cal asked as he swerved to avoid one of the thousands of leaflet purveyors trying to get the attention of wandering tourists.

"Motown Moscow. It's some kind of fusion of Jazz and Communism. Rumor has it that an ex-KGB agent runs the place."

"Motown Moscow? I don't know, Doc. I'm not a huge fan of jazz."

"Come on, Cal. Where's your sense of adventure? Maybe they'll have one of those crazy, frozen vodka bars with Miles Davis playing on top!"

"Okay, okay. But if I get hit on by some seven foot tall Russian troll..."

"Don't worry, man. It'll be fun. I promise to get you home before midnight."

Brian led the way after quickly glancing at his smart phone's mapping app.

+ + +

"You're sure it was him?" Ishi asked into his mobile phone. He listened for the response. "Good. Have the Russians follow and get rid of them."

A pre-emptive strike would impress his father. If things were coming as close to fruition as his father thought, now was the time to take action.

+ + +

"Are you sure we're going the right way? I think we're too far off The Strip, Doc."

"Hold on. Let me check again."

As Brian checked his phone, Cal got the nagging feeling that they were being watched. He casually glanced around, taking in the crowd. Nothing jumped out. Maybe he was tired. Just as he turned back to his friend, he caught someone's eye. The man's gaze lingered a breath too long. Something about the bearded man set off alarm bells in Cal's brain.

"We need to move, now."

Brian looked up from his phone. "Huh?"

"Don't look around. Just act casual. We've got a tail. Bearded giant about forty yards back."

Brian took Cal's cue and followed. They weaved in and out of the packed sidewalk. *Let's see how persistent this guy is*, Cal thought as he quickly turned down a small side street.

As soon as they entered the street, Cal knew he'd made a mistake. What he'd thought was a street was just one of the many service entrances to a casino. No exits unless the back door happened to be open.

"Shit," Cal whispered.

"This is a dead end, Cal."

"I know. Just keep going."

"Why do you think this guy's following us?"

Cal had no idea. Money? Random thuggery?

He stole a quick look back. The bearded giant had materialized with two enormous companions. *Maybe it's time to find out what these guys want.*

Cal nudged Brian and said loudly, "Dude, this isn't the right way!"

Brian took the cue. "Crap! Sorry. I think we turned one street too early."

They swung around and saw that the three giants had quickly closed the gap. Twenty yards separated the two parties.

"Hey, fellas! You guys know how to find Motown Moscow?" Cal asked cheerfully. Maybe the whole thing was a fluke.

Instead of answering, the three men kept walking forward. Their wide frames moved in unison. They fanned out to surround Cal and Brian. As they stepped closer, a van screeched to a halt at the opening of the service alley. The side door banged open and two more men jumped out.

"I guess these guys don't want to talk," Cal mused.

"Yeah. Any ideas?"

"Hey diddle diddle?" It was a private joke. Marines were fond of saying 'Hey diddle diddle, straight up the middle', to explain a full-frontal assault.

Brian nodded and put his hands in his pockets. He gripped his weapons casually. "You sure we can't talk about this guys?"

The bearded giant spoke for the first time in a heavy Russian accent. "No talk. Now we crush you."

"Whatever you say, Ivan Drago. I think..." the words stuck in Cal's throat as he noticed a figure climb over their attackers' van and jump down on the two men waiting for their companions. As he fell, the shaggy stranger pointed two tasers at the backs of his targets. Their muted screams and Cal's gaze drew the attention of the three hulking men. They turned their heads. Cal and Brian took advantage of the distraction and attacked.

Cal unsheathed his knife and dropped into a squat, simultaneously slicing a clean line through the man's left knee. The man screamed in surprise and bent to grab his injured leg. As he did, Cal sprang up pulling the man's head down as he drove his knee up into the Russian's nose. The man collapsed unconscious.

Meanwhile, Brian went to work on the giant on the far right. As a combat veteran, Brian knew there was rarely such thing as a fair fight. Use any advantage you can. Instead of trying to reach a swing at the man's head, Ramirez directed his uppercut at his groin. The man quickly joined his companion on the ground.

The bearded giant was the only one who had a chance to retaliate. As Cal turned back to the last attacker, the wild looking stranger sprang on the larger man and landed a brutal blow to the man's temple with what looked like a short billy club. Game over.

"We need to get out of here," said the longhaired newcomer. Cal noticed that the man was barely breathing heavy. His posture looked almost animalistic in its grace.

Not wanting to wait around for the authorities, Cal agreed. "You lead the way…"

"Daniel."

"You lead the way, Daniel."

The three men rushed to the end of the alley, replacing their weapons as they ran. Once they got to the van, they squeezed around back and disappeared into the moving crowds.

✚ ✚ ✚

After silently following Daniel for fifteen minutes, the trio approached an old apartment complex. Daniel walked up the only flight of stairs and opened the third door.

He ushered his guests inside and turned on the lights.

The apartment was small but spotless. It was sparingly appointed. No pictures, just a small kitchenette, bathroom, an old bed and some books on a shelf. It looked much newer than the exterior.

Daniel took off his trench coat and placed it on the bed neatly. As he did Cal noticed the large tattoo on the man's left arm. It was the trademark skull and arrowhead of Marine sniper units with the motto: 'Swift, silent, deadly.'

"You're a Marine?" Cal asked.

"I was," Daniel answered quietly as he moved to the kitchen sink and washed his hands.

"Me too."

Daniel didn't respond except with a silent nod.

Cal thought of what to say as he studied the other Marine. The young man looked fit and muscular. He probably stood just over six feet with dirty blonde hair and beard. Cal guessed that the guy couldn't be more than thirty years old. *Where'd this guy come from?*

Daniel turned back from the kitchen and spoke. "How'd you get involved with the Russians? Gambling debts?"

Cal was totally confused. "You know those guys?"

"I know WHO they are. They're hired thugs. They split their time between security duty and breaking knee caps," Daniel explained.

"Let's back up a minute, man. First off, I'm Cal and this is my buddy Brian. He was a corpsman so we all call him Doc."

The three men shook hands. "I'm Daniel Briggs."

"I guess we forgot to say thanks, Daniel," Brian added. "How'd you happen to be nearby anyways?"

Daniel took a second to respond. How had he known? How did he ever know where danger was? Some might call it a gift. To Daniel it often felt like a curse. He didn't know how to explain but he tried.

"You guys spend any time over in Iraq or Afghanistan?" he asked.

Both men nodded.

"You ever have a hard time sleeping?"

"I don't, but I have plenty of friends that do," Cal offered.

"Same here," Brian added.

Daniel paused again, praying that he was doing the right thing in telling these strangers about some of his darkest secrets.

"Well, I'm one of the ones that couldn't sleep. Tried alcohol for while. Didn't take. Neither did the prescriptions. Then I found God. Now I help other people."

Brian and Cal looked at each other. Who was this guy? He'd obviously had some post-traumatic issues.

They both knew that a lot of returning veterans had PTSD symptoms. Some of the most successful found healing through counseling and religion.

"So what are you doing on the streets of Las Vegas?" Cal asked.

"Long story short, I felt led here. I'm from Florida. Hopped on a bus one day. Vegas was where my bus ticket ran out. I've spent the last few months doing odd jobs during the day and walking the streets at night. I make sure tourists aren't getting taken advantage of. The thieves and con artists are pretty easy to spot if you know what you're looking for. I've just been waiting."

"Waiting for what?" Cal and Brian asked at the same time.

"Something else. I know God will tell me when it's time to move on."

Cal respected the man's conviction. "So what about those guys tonight? How'd you know they were coming after us?"

"Vegas is actually a pretty small town. Once you've been here for a spell, you start to know the characters. I've seen these guys on collecting duty before. They work for that Japanese-themed hotel behind the Bellagio. Usually it's just two of them. When I saw them tonight, they looked like they were on a mission. I decided to follow. You know the rest," Daniel finished.

Cal and Brian stood silent for a second. So they'd been detected at Zimmer's hotel. But what was the motive? Questions started rolling around in Cal's head. How'd they pick out Cal and Brian? Why come after them now? Who told them? Cal had a sneaking suspicion that Congressman Brandon Zimmer had opened his big fucking mouth. He'd have to have a little talk with the arrogant prick.

Cal filed away his thoughts for later. Back to Daniel Briggs. What do you say to a guy that looks like a crazy mountain man and spends most nights playing hero on the streets of Sin City?

Both friends were obviously curious about the man's past.

"So you were a scout sniper in the Corps?"

"Yeah. I'd never picked up a rifle before boot camp. My drill instructors said I was a natural," Daniel explained without a hint of arrogance. "Once I finished up the School of Infantry in Lejeune, I got picked up to go to sniper school."

"How many tours did you do?" asked Brian.

"Iraq once and three times to Afghanistan. Spent some time with MARSOC too."

So this guy had been around the block a few times. Cal would have to find out some more details from his contact at Headquarters Marine Corps.

"If you don't mind me asking, what was your PTSD trigger?" Brian asked.

It didn't look like Daniel minded the question. If he'd already admitted to having sleeping issues, Brian figured he'd probably open up about the rest. It didn't hurt that Cal and Brian had similar backgrounds: brothers-in-arms.

"It wasn't the killing. I never had a problem with that." He paused to gather his thoughts. "The guys we took down were bad dudes. Most were insurgents from across the border. Some of the best shooting I ever did was over-watch for battalion. I knew I was saving Marines' lives. It was my last tour when things went to shit. Some of our teams were getting attached to special ops groups. They wanted to double the number of snipers they were taking into the zone. So we're on this op in the middle of shitland Afghanistan. Real nasty urban area. Full of Taliban and Al Qaeda fighters. We'd just inserted with a team of four SEALs. As soon as we fast roped to the ground and the helo banks left, insurgents took it out with a couple of RPGs. The SEALs told us to find some high ground to get a better vantage point, and they took off for the insurgent position. We tried to get indirect fire or close air support, but higher wouldn't allow it because of the large civilian population. Me and my spotter got into one of the compounds and found the best view we could. We watched as those SEALs leapfrogged all the way to the enemy pos. It was pitch black, but we could see that two of the guys were already wounded. Those brave sons-a-bitches kept assaulting and cussing out higher over the radio. I'd just setup my Barrett .50 cal as I watched all four SEALs get mowed down by a truck-mounted machine gun. I started unloading on the fuckers. It was like shooting fish in a barrel. They kept streaming out, trying to get the bodies of our SEALs."

"Pretty soon they realized where our shots were coming from. They turned their fire on us. I have no idea how long I was shooting. My spotter, Grant, got hit in the shoulder almost right away. He kept calling out shots though. Finally some fucker gets smart and they start lobbing mortar rounds at us. We started pulling back into one of the only two story buildings in the area. Grant was wounded but still doing okay. Then he got hit with an AK round in the leg. Went right through his femur. Blood everywhere. I lugged my .50 cal on one shoulder and dragged Grant under the other arm. We get in the bottom floor of this building and all hell broke loose. It sounded like two or three mortar tubes thumping rounds onto us. We somehow got to the lowest part of the building before it collapsed."

"I don't know how I didn't get crushed. Grant did though. His other leg was completely smashed under the rubble. Grant tried not to scream as his leg pumped more and more blood onto the dirt floor. I applied a quick tourniquet and tried to make him comfortable. I remember telling him that someone would be there soon. Man, was I wrong."

"For the next two days we listened quietly as the insurgents searched the rubble pile. I don't know how they didn't get to us. I could even hear the fuckers cheering. Found out later that they'd mutilated the SEALs' bodies and hung 'em up outside where we were trapped."

"Our radio got lost in the explosion, so we were shit out of luck there. I kept telling Grant that we just had to stay quiet and some of our boys would be there soon. He was delirious with pain for a day. I tried to keep him awake but he finally passed out. A day later, I couldn't find a pulse."

"He died in my arms. We'd been friends since boot camp. I was the best man at his wedding. I barely had a scratch on me. A day later, I heard a lot of firing and then troops talking English. I screamed and screamed until they pinpointed where I was. They brought in the engineers and got us out. I found out later that the enemy had been waiting for us. Apparently some American politician had opened his mouth and word got to the right people on the other side. We didn't have a chance."

"I spent a lot of time afterwards wondering why. I'd drink my way into a dark tunnel and wonder: why not me instead of Grant? Why did he have to leave his wife and kid? Why do politicians leak secrets? The answer I found was simple: It's not up to me. The Man upstairs has some kind of plan. Maybe he was saving me for something. All I can do now is try my best and live up to the second chance."

Cal and Brian stood quietly, digesting the story.

"So how do you sleep now?" asked Cal.

"Like a baby most nights. I still have bad dreams every once in a while. Mostly they're memories of Grant slowly dying in my arms, repeating his wife's name over and over. He looks more like an angel in my dreams now."

"I appreciate you telling us. We've been in the shit a few times, too. How about you come have a drink with us so we can thank you properly?" asked Cal.

"I don't drink alcohol anymore, but sure. How about tomorrow night?"

They exchanged contact information and Cal promised to call Daniel the next day to confirm. Cal and Brian said their goodbyes and walked outside.

"You think we should change our hotel room now?" Brian asked sarcastically.

Chapter 16
Las Vegas, Nevada
9:30pm, September 16th

THE LARGE BEARDED RUSSIAN stood almost at attention. Ishi Nakamura paced back and forth in front of the giant.

"How is it that you let these two men get away?" Ishi asked once again.

"I told you, Mr. Nakamura. We were not expecting the third man. We aslo did not know the capabilities of the targets. That information could have been useful. I now have two men in hospital," grumbled the hired thug.

"I don't care about your men, you idiot. We pay you a lot of money to take care of such simple tasks. I still can't believe five military-trained men couldn't take down two targets," Ishi continued as he paced.

"Technically, it was three m…"

"Shut up! Just shut up!" Ishi screamed. "Now I want you to be ready the next time I call. If you need to find more men, do it. Meanwhile, I'll clean up this mess."

Ishi dreaded the next conversation with his father. Nakamura-san would not be amused.

Cal and Brian called Neil as soon as they left Daniel's apartment. He'd get them another suite at the Venetian by the time they packed their gear. It was a little farther away, but owned by a friend of the company.

"The reservation will be under your Alpha aliases," Neil instructed. Each operator at SSI was assigned three aliases (Alpha, Bravo and Charlie) for contingencies. "I suggest you boys get some rest for tomorrow."

"Thanks, Dad," Cal retorted. "We'll see you tomorrow, Neil."

He replaced the phone in his pocket and followed Brian through the door at the Cosmopolitan.

"You still happy you tagged along, Doc?"

"Who me? I'm used to your crazy adventures by now, man. What's next? Naked stripper assassins parachuting through our glass windows at the Venetian?" quipped Brian.

"I sure as hell hope not. You'd be too distracted by the naked girls to defend yourself."

"Very funny, jackass."

They got in and out of their room quickly. There really hadn't been time to unpack so grabbing their bags was easy. Cal put the Do Not Disturb sign on the outside of the door. They'd let the reservation run its course for the next two days, just in case.

Cal led the way down the back staircase and headed for the service exit.

Daniel Briggs knelt next to his bed. The adrenaline finally seeped from his system; he was exhausted but happy. He took a moment to say a quick prayer. When he finished, he stripped down to his boxer briefs and fell right to sleep.

Chapter 17
Las Vegas, Nevada
7:08am, September 17th

CONGRESSMAN ZIMMER AND MSgt Trent arrived late the night before. It was a bright morning that promised to be clear and beautiful. Not a cloud in the sky.

Zimmer padded into the living area just after 7:00am wearing some gym shorts and a t-shirt. Trent had to admit that the man didn't look like a pansy. He seemed to be in good shape. Maybe in another life he could've been in the military.

Trent was shirtless but already dressed in gym shorts and running shoes. He'd sprawled his massive frame over the long couch overlooking the outdoor pool. Creeping up on the big four oh, Willy Trent was still as fit as any professional athlete. At one time, he'd been drafted into the NFL. He soon found another calling with the Marines.

"You sleep okay, Top?"

"Just fine, sir."

"You ready to hit the gym in a few minutes?"

"Yes, sir. I'll throw on a t-shirt and we can go."

Both men finished getting ready then headed to the workout facility.

An hour later, they headed back to their suite.

"I don't know about you, Top, but I needed that," stated a completely sweat-soaked Zimmer.

"Yes, sir. Always nice to start the day off with a good workout."

"What time are we meeting Cal this morning?"

Trent looked at his watch. "He called while we were in the gym and pushed it back an hour. Apparently they had a little situation last night. He's trying to get a read on it before we meet."

"What kind of situation?" asked Zimmer.

Trent shrugged. "He wouldn't tell me over the phone. I guess we'll find out soon enough."

Getting back to their suite, each man split off to their respective rooms to shower and change.

Brandon was putting his pants on when his personal cell phone rang. He looked down at the caller ID.

"Hey, Dad."

"How are things going, Son?"

"We got in last night. We'll be meeting Cal soon."

"Good. Any progress on their investigation?" the Senator asked.

"I'm not sure yet. I'll know more after we meet, I think."

"Now you remember, Son. Let those boys do their job. From what I hear, they're very good at what they do."

"I know, Dad. I'll behave."

"Call me when you know more," Senator Zimmer instructed.

The line went dead. Brandon tucked the phone into his pocket and finishing dressing. Zimmer hoped it would be an uneventful day.

MSgt Trent led the way down to the lobby. He scanned the area and ushered the Congressman toward the main exit. Just as they were about to step into the revolving doors, someone called out.

"Brandon!"

Trent and Zimmer turned around. Ishi Nakamura approached with a pair of security guards. Zimmer plastered a happy look on his face and waved to his old friend.

"Hey, Ishi."

Nakamura walked up and hugged him. "How come you didn't call me when you got in? I would've sent up some champagne or something."

"It was late when we got in last night. I didn't want to bother you."

"You're never a bother, my friend. Remember, you are MY responsibility."

Trent detected a slight flare of a threat in Nakamura's tone.

"God, I'm sorry, Ishi. I forgot to introduce you to my new bodyguard. Willy Trent, this is my old friend, Ishi Nakamura."

The two men shook hands. "Good to meet you, Mr. Trent. Can I call you Willy?" Ishi asked pleasantly.

"Mr. Trent would be just fine, sir."

Ishi's face fell for a split second. He recovered and said, "Once a Marine, always a Marine, eh, Mr. Trent?"

"That's right, sir. You can take the man out of the Marines, but you can't take the Marine out of the man."

Ishi laughed. "Ha! I like that. Either way, welcome to Las Vegas and let us know if the hotel's security team can help in any way."

Ishi turned to Congressman Zimmer. "Brandon, I've got some people I'd like you to meet later today. They're big donors and are helping with the planning for the Democratic National Convention. How about we grab dinner tonight?"

Zimmer looked to Trent who nodded. "Sounds good. What time should we meet you down here?"

"Let's make it seven thirty."

"Alright, we'll see you then."

The two men shook hands again and went their separate ways. As Nakamura passed the concierge desk, his phone buzzed. He picked it up.

Ishi answered in Japanese. "Did you see your target?"

"Yes."

"Good. Make sure he's taken before my dinner with the Congressman. I want no mistakes."

"Yes, Nakamura-san."

Ishi ended the call and continued to his office. *It's time to teach Brandon a little lesson.*

Trent hailed a cab and held the door open for Zimmer. Five minutes later, they were getting out in front of Caesar's Palace. During the ride, Trent spotted two vehicles following them from the hotel.

"Sir, I'm gonna need you to do exactly as I say," Trent murmured to Zimmer.

"Huh? What's going on?" he whispered back.

"Just keep walking toward the main entrance over there. Don't look around. We've got a tail."

"Is it someone from the hotel?" Zimmer asked calmly.

"Yes. Now we're gonna do a little extra walking. Follow me."

Trent slipped in front of Zimmer and started weaving his way through the morning crowd. Brandon followed closely.

Willy pulled out his phone and dialed Cal.

"Yeah?" Cal answered.

"We've got extra friends trying to wreck the party. Let's move to the backup location."

"I'll see you there."

Trent pulled his phone away from his ear and walked faster. Zimmer was having a hard time not running just to match the Marine's long stride. They walked quickly around the curved drive. Trent walked up to a cab and hopped in, Zimmer right behind.

Willy instructed the driver to go to Circus Circus at the north end of the The Strip.

"What the hell is going on?" Zimmer whispered.

"I think your friend Ishi sent some of his goons after us. Not sure if it's just to keep an eye on us or what. I didn't want to take any chances."

"Should we even go back to the hotel later?"

"What choice do we have? Let's focus on getting to this meeting first. Maybe Cal will have something for us." Trent continued to watch behind them. He couldn't pinpoint anyone following, but that didn't matter. He'd learned long ago to trust his sixth sense. Right now it was blaring like a foghorn.

Ten minutes later, the cab pulled out of the congested corridor and pulled up in front of the aged Circus Circus. Trent paid the driver then followed Zimmer over to the front entrance.

"We're supposed to meet Cal and Brian in front of the Krispy Kreme stand in the Slots of Fun side of the casino. Stay close now, Congressman."

No sooner had they stepped off towards the entrance that they both felt a pinch on their necks. At first, Trent thought it was a horse fly bite. That was until Zimmer collapsed to the pavement. A large limousine pulled up beside them. The last thing Trent saw before he fell unconscious was the rushed steps of four men running his way.

"Where the hell are they?" Cal thought out loud.

"Have you tried calling him again?" Brian asked.

"Yeah. Three times. There's no way Top left his phone in the hotel room."

"Want me to go outside and take a look?"

"No. Let's both go. Maybe they just got caught in traffic."

As they walked, Cal texted Neil to track the GPS locator in Trent's phone. All SSI phones were rigged for tracking.

They stepped out into the sunlight and looked around. No sign of Trent and the Congressman. Cal's phone buzzed.

"What did you find, Neil?"

"The locator says Trent is standing right in front of the main entrance to Circus Circus."

"Hold on. Let me walk that way."

Cal pushed past a group of drunken gamblers and headed to the front of the casino.

"Do you see him?" Neil asked.

"Not yet. You sure you've got it right?"

"I'm showing a full signal. No way this thing is wrong."

Cal started jogging. His anxiety increased as he reached the sidewalk leading into the building. Both men looked all around.

"Cal, look!" Brian was pointing at the ground.

Lying on the ground next to a pair of broken sunglasses was MSgt Trent's cell phone.

"Holy shit. Neil, message Trav and have him send in the contingency team."

Cal ended the call and sprinted to catch a cab.

Chapter 18
Camp Spartan, Arrington, TN
12:16pm, September 17th

TRAVIS HADEN ADDRESSED his three closest advisors: Todd Dunn, Marge Haines, and Dr. Higgins, SSI's resident psychologist. He'd just run through the details from Cal.

"So, Cal just called for the contingency team. I think we better prep for the worst. Any questions?"

Marge Haines started, "What do we have on books as far as Trent's security with Zimmer?"

"I can answer that," Todd Dunn said. "We tasked him out as a VIP security contract. By the way, I just got confirmation that the contingency team is in the air."

"Good," Travis nodded. "What else?"

"Who else knew about the security arrangement?" Haines asked.

Dunn shrugged. "We'll have to assume that Zimmer's immediate support staff knows. Senator Zimmer is also in the loop."

Dr. Higgins raised his hand. "Have you thought about a possible leak, Travis?"

"I've thought about it, but don't have a clue who it could be."

"I think it's fair to assume that the operation has been compromised and we're dealing with a larger threat than we initially believed," Higgins intoned professionally.

"I think you're right, Doc. First, Cal tells me about getting attacked by these giant Russians. Now, Top and Zimmer are gone. I think we need to alert the Council and start putting some more pieces into play."

"Is it time to involve the authorities?" Haines asked.

"Let's give Cal a little time. I find it hard to believe that this Japanese group would dispose of Zimmer so soon. I think something else is brewing," Travis said.

"I concur," agreed Dr. Higgins. "It looks like our new enemy is taking extreme measures to keep us out of the picture. Do we have any thoughts on their motive other than to blackmail Congressman Zimmer?"

"Neil's working on it right now. I think Cal said he was close to getting into the Ichiban system," answered Travis.

"Seems like a long time for Neil to crack the code," Dunn noted.

"Yeah. I think these Ichiban guys have some serious horsepower under the hood. I'm not liking it," answered Travis. "Let's meet up again in an hour. Maybe we'll have some good news from Vegas by then."

Congressman Zimmer woke up to a splitting headache. He tried to open his eyes but realized they were covered by a blindfold. His arms were numb and bound to the chair he was tied to. *Where the hell am I?*

He tried to shift into a more comfortable position and heard a chair squeak.

"Hello?" Zimmer croaked. He noticed his throat was bone dry.

"I thought we talked about expectations, Brandon?"

"Ishi?"

"Yes. I don't think you understand the position you've put me in. We saved you from public embarrassment and possibly life in jail. You repay us by ignoring our rules and taking advantage of our friendship," Ishi explained smoothly.

"What the hell are you talking about, man?"

"Let's start with your bodyguard. If you were worried about personal security, why didn't you contact someone within your government?" Ishi asked.

"No one listens to a first-term Congressman. They'd think I was just being paranoid."

"Okay. So why didn't you ask us for additional security?"

Zimmer almost laughed. He might be a little naïve, but he wasn't stupid.

"Look man, I know I owe you guys a lot, but this is ridiculous. I'm sorry if I broke the rules. If I'd known how much of a problem it would be, I wouldn't have hired Trent."

"Well, you won't have to worry about Master Sergeant Trent anymore."

Brandon's stomach went to his throat.

"What did you do with him, Ishi?"

"Oh, you'll see him soon enough. He's being employed in a more...entertaining way. Are you almost ready for dinner?"

"Tell me where Trent is, Ishi."

"ENOUGH! I'm not the little punk you knew at Harvard, *Congressman*. You can't push me around anymore. From now on you do exactly as I say. Is that understood?"

Brandon knew he couldn't win this fight. He decided to keep his mouth shut and bide his time. At the moment, his own safety didn't seem so important. His main thought as Ishi untied his arms was: *Where is Willy Trent?*

+ + +

MSgt Trent opened his eyes. Where was Zimmer? He quickly surveyed his surroundings. His prison cell was a small windowless room. The space was about ten by ten, the floor concrete. They'd laid him on an old cot with a thin, musty mattress. Trent struggled to his feet. His head pounded. What the hell had they knocked him out with? He remembered the last seconds before passing out. He remembered Zimmer going down. *Where the hell is he?*

Once his mind cleared, he realized they'd taken his clothes. The only thing covering his extensive frame was a stylish loincloth. His captors had also attached a thick collar around his neck. *What the hell?* He flexed his neck and felt around the edges of the leather collar. It felt completely locked in place. Trent thought he detected a small antenna on it as well.

Take a deep breath and think, Willy.

Over the years he'd been in some strange situations. This one was definitely taking the cake. He must look like an overgrown Zulu warrior right now. What was next? A spear and shield? *Someone's gonna pay for this shit.*

As he pondered payback, a robotic voice sparked to life from a hidden speaker.

"In ten minutes, you will be escorted to the weapons room."

"Say what?" Willy yelled back at the faceless voice.

"Prepare yourself."

There were no further instructions. Trent stood baffled. What the hell was going on?

+++

Congressman Zimmer's clothes were waiting for him. Following Ishi's instructions, he changed and used the bathroom to clean up. They'd given him five minutes.

Five minutes later a Japanese man, dressed in a butler's uniform, entered the room.

"Congressman Zimmer, Nakamura-san has requested your presence." The man bowed waiting for a response.

"Okay. I'm, uh, I'm ready to go."

Zimmer followed the man through a short maze of doorways. He occasionally glimpsed a window. The night outside was pitch black. The building felt part industrial part high-end hotel. Where were they? He never saw an exterior door. No easy way out.

Reaching the end of the hallway, the butler opened a heavy oak door. He held it for the Congressman who stepped in alone.

"Ah, here he is!" Zimmer recognized Ishi's voice in the dimly lit room. He looked around and found himself in an elegantly appointed dining room. A group of older Asian gentlemen were gathered near a large plate-glass window.

Brandon put on his best politician smile and stepped into the gloom. "Hey, Ishi."

The men in the corner stopped talking and stared at the freshman Congressman from Massachusetts. *Who are these guys?* They were giving him the creeps with the way they looked at him.

"Congressman Zimmer, please let me introduce you to my father and some of his associates," Ishi said loud enough for the room to hear.

Brandon followed Ishi to the group. He went to glance at the large window, but the light beyond flicked off as if on command.

"Father, this is my good friend Congressman Zimmer."

Kazuo Nakamura stepped forward and shook Zimmer's hand. "It is a pleasure to finally meet you, Congressman. My son has told me so much about you." He smiled almost conspiratorially.

"Please, Mr. Nakamura, call me Brandon."

"Very well." He turned to his associates. "I won't bother to tell you all their names, but let me introduce you. These men are my closest friends. They are all captains of industry and leaders of Japan. We trace our family roots back to the days of the samurai, through the rise of our Empire during the Second World War, and now Japan's rebuilding. Together we've known both loss and success. In short, they are as close as family."

"It's very nice to meet you all," Brandon said respectfully.

"Do you enjoy hand-to-hand combat, Brandon?" asked Ishi's father.

"I've watched a little Mixed Martial Arts on television. It's okay," Brandon answered.

Kazuo Nakamura chuckled. "Ah yes. Your country calls it MMA. Well, what we have tonight is MUCH more exciting than your MMA. Can Ishi get you something to drink, Brandon?"

"Uh, sure."

Congressman Zimmer's mind swirled. He had a sinking feeling about the night's festivities.

+ + +

A buzz sounded and the door to MSgt Trent's cell opened. No one entered.

"Follow the hallway to the left and enter the weapons room," the voice overhead ordered.

"Sure would be nice if you said please," Trent shot back. When he didn't get a response he entered the illuminated hallway. He walked slowly toward the weapons room. At set intervals he could now see other cell doors and video cameras installed above. Trent waved to the cameras and kept walking.

Reaching the only other open door, he peeked in. Inside was an impressive array of weapons displayed in stainless steel racks. Not the typical weapons Trent was used to seeing in armories. There were no firearms. All types of swords, spears, and tridents waited on one side of the space. The other side housed shields of varying sizes, along with nets. There were two of everything. Trent whistled quietly and looked up at the closest camera.

"Impressive shit you have here, fellas."

"You have five minutes to arm. Take your weapons of choice and make your way to the door at the other side of the room," the voice ordered.

Trent surveyed the racks. Being a lead instructor at SSI, he had experience with a multitude of arms. That included weapons of opportunity; everything from lead pipes to broken beer bottles. He finally found what he wanted. Ignoring the larger items, he picked up two identical blades. *Fuck it. If I'm going out, I'm going down swinging with a couple KA-BARs, baby.* The former Marine Master Sergeant took an overhand grip on both.

He cracked his neck to both sides, shook the tension out of his arms and legs, walked to the opposite end of the room and waited.

Congressman Zimmer tried to be cordial as he mingled with the group of successful Japanese elders. He couldn't put his finger on it, but it felt like they were subtly trying get his take on the American economy. There were little comments like: "Would you say the dollar is more favorable than the Euro?" "What will new housing starts be next quarter?" "Will Congress re-examine its stance on internet gaming?"

Taken separately and outside the current situation, they might be innocent questions. He'd heard them all before. And yet, he sensed a well-concealed urgency in their tone. What the hell were they after?

These were men of substance. All seemed to have a fierce determination lying beneath their passive facial expressions.

A quiet gong rang from some unseen corner.

"Gentlemen, please direct your attention to the arena. Our festivities are about to begin," the white-haired butler announced.

Congressman Zimmer followed the excitedly murmuring crowd to the large window. As he found a spot, the area beyond the glass slowly illuminated. The arena was about one floor below their vantage point. It looked like a smaller version of the gladiatorial rings he'd seen in Italy. The floor was even covered in sand. *What the hell is this?* Zimmer thought.

Kazuo Nakamura made his way over to Brandon, with Ishi in tow. He addressed Zimmer in a measured tone.

"What you are about to see is usually reserved for our private enjoyment. You see we were all warriors in our past lives. Now we must feel the sting of a blade or the blunt side of a shield vicariously through others. This facility was built especially for such events. We felt that in your current...situation...it might be useful to have you enjoy this as well."

Nakamura turned to the butler and nodded. The servant pressed a small button on the wall and a door in the arena opened. Zimmer watched as a huge man entered the small arena. From his vantage point, Brandon could swear the man stood almost eight feet tall. He was covered head-to-toe in tattoos. In his right arm, he carried an enormous spiked club over his shoulder. Turning to the viewing window, the behemoth bowed.

His host explained, "The warrior you see below is a very special part of my family. Years ago, we established a sort of an orphanage on the island of Samoa. We took very good care of the orphans. The children were rarely placed with new families and most became employees within our companies as they aged. Some, like this man, are recognized for their fighting prowess. We start them in combat training from the age of seven. This one, he calls himself Poktoo, has an amazing proficiency for killing. He has never been bested. What do you think of my Poktoo, Brandon?"

"He's very, uh, large," Brandon answered hesitantly. He wanted nothing to do with the huge fighter.

Nakamura laughed aloud. "Indeed he is, Brandon. Now would you like to see our other fighter?"

"Sure, I guess."

Nakamura nodded again to the butler who pressed another button. The door opposite Poktoo slid open and another warrior exited. This dark-skinned man looked large as well, but not even close to the enormity of the first fighter. Zimmer looked closer and inhaled quickly. *Holy crap! That's Trent!*

"As you now see, Brandon, that is your friend William Trent. Not only did we want you to be entertained..." Nakamura paused for effect, "...we also wanted this to be a lesson of what can happen if our instructions are not followed in the future."

Congressman Zimmer could only watch in horror as Trent paced into the center of the sandy arena and prepared for battle.

The door to the arena slid open and Trent peered in. *So now I'm a damned gladiator. The boys at home will never believe this one.*

He stepped into the ring and tested the sand. It wasn't very deep but it would impede quick movement. Trent looked across the arena at his opponent. *That's one big dude. Maybe I should've brought more than my KA-BARs.*

The huge tattooed guy was looking up at the big window waiting for something. *I guess that's our audience. I wonder when they're gonna tell us to...* Trent couldn't even finish his thought as a loud GONG sounded and the monster charged.

"Hey, Cal, I've got something!" Neil yelled into the next room.

Cal sprang up from his laptop and ran into the living room.

"What's up?"

"After I got into the Ichiban system, I started trying to pinpoint anything that might help us. I still can't get into their super secure stuff, but I was able to hack into their logistics software."

"How does that help us?"

"Well, their logistics package deals with everything from ordering toilet paper to tasking employees."

"Come on, Neil. Get to the point."

"Sorry. Okay, so one of the things they track is their transportation system. Apparently they have a fleet of automobiles ranging from delivery trucks to stretch limos. They'd built this thing so that when an order goes into the system, the schedule is automatically synced with the smart phone of the first available driver."

"How again does this help us?"

"In order to complete the request, the input must include a start and finish destination. I'm looking at today's requests and there've been one hundred and thirty-two. Sixteen of those requests start at different locations but end up at the same destination."

Cal's impatience was visibly growing.

"We don't have time for this, Neil. How does that help me find our guys?"

"I'm almost there. The destination of these sixteen requests is at this location, about twenty miles outside of Las Vegas." Neil pointed to a map on one of his computer screens. "I'm not finding any hotels or amenities in the general vicinity. The only thing public records show is some industrial property owned by a subsidiary of Ichiban Gaming, LLC."

"You sure about this?"

"I mean, I can't confirm that our boys are there, but it seems like a good place to start."

Cal thought for a minute. If they went into some industrial complex, guns blazing, the local police would be all over them.

"How long would it take us to drive there?" Cal asked.

"It's almost 8:00pm so I'd say...thirty minutes, forty max."

"Okay. Message the contingency team and tell them to get in their vehicles and meet me in the parking garage in five minutes. I'll grab Brian and take him with me."

"You want me to come?" Neil asked hopefully.

"No. I'll need you here to help coordinate and break everything down if this thing goes to shit. Remember what we discussed, priority goes to keeping SSI out of the papers," instructed Cal.

He didn't wait for Neil's response. Running to the bedroom, he grabbed his .45 with three extra magazines and stowed them in his sport coat. Grabbing his keys off the side table, he bolted for the door.

✦ ✦ ✦

He'd already briefed his four team leaders. In addition to Cal and Brian, there were sixteen men waiting to step off. They piled back into their four vehicles, a mixed bag of standard rentals armed with silenced weapons and a variety of breaching equipment.

"How sure is Neil that this is the place?" Brian asked Cal.

"I'd say around ninety percent. It's really all we have so we've gotta go."

Cal started the car and pulled out of the parking spot. Every vehicle had the target address programmed into a GPS. They would each take slightly different routes. No need to be a bigger target than necessary.

They pulled onto Las Vegas Boulevard. The streets were jammed with revelers. It was imperative that they get off the main drag quickly. Cal's small strike force could be stuck for an hour on the packed thoroughfare if they weren't careful.

The politician handed his boarding pass to the airline attendant. It would be a nice flight out to Las Vegas. First class was always comfortable. The flight would probably be the last he'd ever take on a commercial airliner. Next stop: Air Force One.

+ + +

The huge Samoan bellowed and swung a wide sweeping blow at Trent's head. Willy barely had time to duck and roll to the side. *This guy is fast.* Trent thought.

His opponent completed the swing with a graceful 360 degree spin. *Must be some island fighting style.*

Poktoo growled and looked at Trent. I'll bet he's used to killing dudes with the first swing.

The trick with big boys was to either take out their legs or take them out from afar. He didn't have a gun so he'd have to take it close. Unless...

Trent rushed Poktoo with some tentative downward stabs at the man's midsection. He needed to get the man off-balance. Willy roared as he tried to sweep his enemy's left leg. Their shins connected and...nothing. The Marine looked up in shock as the tattooed devil grinned down. Before Trent could react, the deadly club came up, butt end first, and slammed him in the chin.

Willy flew back, the darkness threatening to overtaken him. He heard muted cheers from the observation deck as he struggled to his feet.

He stumbled back and shook away the stars. *Okay, shithead. No more games.*

Poktoo had taken the time during Trent's stumble to throw his arms up in a victorious roar. As he looked back down at Trent, the former Marine cocked the KA-BAR in his right hand and stepped into a powerful throw. Willy knew from experience that the KA-BAR wasn't the most balanced throwing knife. As luck would have it, he'd recently won a few bucks off former Delta guys at SSI. They'd bragged about their hot shit knife throwing skills. They used some little blades that were about as big as a man's hand. Being a Marine and sick of their bragging, Trent insisted on using a KA-BAR. After hours of practice, he'd perfected his throws with the larger blade. He could hit the bull's-eye on a log target fifteen yards away. Poktoo was maybe five yards from him.

The giant Samoan barely had time to register surprise as the razor sharp blade entered his open mouth and entered his brain stem. His eyes opened wide as he crumpled to the floor.

"One shot, one kill, motherfucker. Oorah," Trent mumbled.

He turned around and yelled at the observation window. "You got another one, assholes?!"

The robotic voice returned. "Congratulations, champion. Drop your weapon and proceed to the open door."

Trent looked toward the door that was even now sliding open. He decided enough was enough. Switching the remaining KA-BAR from his left to right hand, Willy threw the weapon at the window. He heard a muffled yell as the blade bounced harmlessly off the reinforced glass.

Instead of further instruction from the speaker, Trent heard a beep on his large collar. For the second time that day, he collapsed unconscious as an electric charge mercilessly racked his body.

+ + +

As the KA-BAR entered his champion's mouth, Kazuo Nakamura screamed in rage. "NO!!"

Zimmer's concern for Trent was replaced with barely concealed exultation. Considering the circumstances, it seemed like such a small victory, but a victory nonetheless.

"Order that man to his cell now!" Nakamura screamed.

The invisible voice did as instructed. That was when Trent decided to throw his knife at the spectators. Brandon almost laughed out loud as, collectively, the men all ducked.

There were angry shouts as they directed their ire at Kazuo Nakamura. Zimmer couldn't understand anything they said, but he got the sense that they were like a crowd who'd paid good money for a prize fight and then watched a ten second knockout.

Nakamura and his son tried to calm the heated guests. Soon they were ushered out of the observation room and into waiting vehicles by apologetic staff. Zimmer followed behind and watched. As the powerful men were loaded into their respective vehicles, a small troop of beautiful women exited the industrial building and filed in with them. Doors closed and the limos departed. *What the...?*

"Brandon."

Zimmer turned around and found Ishi waiting next to a Cadillac Escalade. "It's time to head back to the hotel. I'll drive."

Congressman Zimmer nodded and moved to get in. He stepped up to Ishi. "What are you going to do with Trent?"

"He'll stay alive as long as he's winning."

Zimmer nodded and looked down at his shoes. Without thinking, he cocked his right arm and slugged Ishi in the temple. His former friend collapsed to the ground. Zimmer shook the tingling out of his hand and waited to see if Ishi would get up. He didn't.

I've gotta get Trent. With a quick glance around, Congressman Brandon Zimmer ran for the building's open door. He didn't have a plan, but he couldn't leave the Marine behind.

Chapter 19
Outskirts of Las Vegas, Nevada
8:25pm, September 17th

"**WE'RE ABOUT TWO** minutes out," Cal announced as he looked at his watch. He felt a sense of dread that they might be too late. He never should have let Zimmer and Trent out of his sight. Maybe if he'd put some kind of tracking device on them, then just maybe... No. He couldn't start thinking that way. Trent was a big boy and more than capable of handling the assignment. They'd all underestimated the threat.

Cal pulled up to the rendezvous point. It was in a small depression just off the narrow two-lane highway. One of the other teams was already there and had spread into a hasty security perimeter. The hiding spot was about two hundred yards from the target building. The plan was to get eyes on it, see if they could detect the presence of their two missing members, and then act accordingly.

The operation had to be fast. No one wanted the local authorities in the picture. SSI couldn't afford the publicity.

"Any updates?" Cal asked the team leader on station. He was a small Hispanic with a long beard that he liked to braid into dual strands. Everyone called him Gaucho, sort of a Spanish version of a cowboy. The man was a former Delta operator and carefully reckless, hence the nickname.

"We got here about five minutes ago. Saw ten to fifteen stretch limos buggin' out from the other side of the building. Couldn't make out Top in the crowd."

"Any signs of life in the building?"

Gaucho shook his head. "Haven't been able to tell. You want us to go take a look, boss?"

Cal peered into darkness. "The other teams will be here in a second. I don't want to waste time waiting on recon. How about you head over there with your boys and scope things out? We'll be right behind you."

"Got it, boss." Gaucho rushed back to his team and gave hushed instructions. The group of four took off at a jog. They knew what to do.

Two minutes later, the remaining teams pulled up. Cal gave the men a quick rundown of the scheme of maneuver. A minute later, the small assault force spread across the barren terrain, anxious to find out the fate of MSgt Trent.

+ + +

Zimmer didn't see anyone in the hallway. He didn't know where to go, but he correctly assumed that the holding cells were on the lower level. Running, he tried opening each door he reached. Every one was locked.

After a couple minutes of random wandering, Brandon stopped and got his bearings. *I don't have much time*, he thought. Just then, the butler from the observation room exited one of the hallway doors.

"Congressman, how may I help you?"

Well, at least they haven't alerted the security staff yet.

"I, uh, think I left my cell phone up in the observation room." The excuse sounded lame but the man seemed to believe it.

"I would be happy to get it and bring it to you in your vehicle, sir," the butler replied respectfully.

"That's okay. Just point me the right way and I'll grab it." Zimmer tried to act as nonchalant as possible. The last thing he needed was to have the butler in tow.

"I am afraid that it not possible, Congressman. Visitors cannot travel alone inside the building. Now if I can escort you outside..."

Zimmer's patience ran out. Instead of letting the man finish, he closed the gap and delivered a vicious uppercut into the unsuspecting man's stomach. The butler doubled over. Zimmer caught him on the way to the floor and propped him up against the wall.

"Now you listen to me," Zimmer whispered into the man's ear. "You take me to my friend right fucking now."

The man still struggled to breathe but nodded his head. Zimmer felt remotely guilty for assaulting the aged servant, but he didn't have many options at the time.

"Which way?" asked Zimmer.

His captive pointed to the door he'd just exited.

"Is it locked?"

The man nodded.

"Give me the key," ordered Zimmer.

Half bent, the butler obliged by giving the Congressman a key ring and indicating which one to use. Zimmer grabbed the key with his right hand and the back of the man's collar with his left. Half dragging his guide, Brandon unlocked the door and moved inside.

Ishi came to. Lying just outside the open door of the Escalade, he struggled to get his bearings. He suddenly remembered Zimmer's fist connecting with his head. *Shit! Where is Zimmer?*

The younger Nakamura rose and looked around frantically. His vision was still blurry and he stumbled back against his vehicle. Just as he regained his balance, he looked up and saw what looked like a line of men approaching the building from about fifty yards away. Was he seeing things? The men jogged closer and Ishi panicked.

Jumping into the driver's seat, he started the large SUV, put it in drive, and gunned the gas. He squealed out of the parking lot as he fumbled for his cell phone.

✚ ✚ ✚

"Shit. Who was that?" Cal asked in a whisper. No answer came. He knew time was up. The first team to the building had already reported seeing employees through the upper level windows of the large industrial complex. They'd approached from the opposite side and found a door. Gaucho had already taken care of the lock with his pick set.

Cal didn't like going in blind, but what choice did they have?

The teams stacked up just outside of the unlocked door. Cal nodded to Gaucho, who winked back.

The small man opened the door quickly and the teams filed in, weapons drawn.

✚ ✚ ✚

Miraculously, Zimmer and the butler didn't run into any other staff on the way to the holding cells. What Brandon didn't know was that after the commotion of the fight, Trent was swiftly thrown unconscious into his cell and the remaining security staff had run upstairs to assist the unsettled guests. They'd then been tasked with riding along as an added precaution. The building was, therefore, currently undermanned.

Zimmer stepped up to Trent's cell. To the right of the door was a small red button that the butler said would open the portal. Brandon pressed it and looked inside. Trent had been unceremoniously tossed just inside the door. He seemed to be stirring.

"Top!" Zimmer whispered as loudly as he dared.

Trent turned his head slowly and looked at Zimmer through foggy eyes. "That you, Congressman?" he croaked.

"Yeah. Can you make it through the door? I don't want this damned thing to lock us both in."

The tough Marine nodded and got to all fours. He bear crawled through the doorway. Once out, Zimmer grabbed the butler, shoved him into the room, and closed the door. He double-checked just to make sure the lock was secured.

"Do you think you can walk?"

"Yeah." Trent stood on slightly shaky knees and shook his head. "I've gotta get this collar off. I could live without another one of those shocks."

Despite the gravity of the situation, Zimmer chuckled. "Come on. Let's get out of here."

Zimmer led the way, still not running into any Japanese personnel.

"Where did everyone go?" Trent asked.

"I don't know. I think...did you hear that?" Zimmer whispered.

Trent nodded and nudged his way into the lead. They could see a bend just ahead. It sounded like muted footsteps coming their way.

"Let's go find out who that is."

Zimmer looked at the huge black man, still wearing only a loincloth. "You think that's a good idea, Top?"

"Trust me, Congressman. Whoever that is, they're in for a world of hurt." Trent cracked his knuckles and sprinted off toward the bend.

The assault team hadn't run into any resistance. While that seemed odd, no man complained. They'd searched most of the lower level. Eventually they came to a section that looked older yet well-maintained. Gaucho looked back at Cal for direction. Cal gave a thumbs-up.

They moved swiftly down the corridor, checking doors as they went. All were locked and there didn't seem to be any need to open them yet. They approached a bend as Gaucho signaled the group to stop. Listening carefully, they clearly heard something. Was that bare feet running their way? Weapons readied, the elite team of SSI operators waited calmly for the approaching runner. The sound got closer when all of a sudden, MSgt Willy Trent, resplendent in his stylish loincloth, rounded the corner and skidded to a halt in front of Gaucho.

"Well I'll be damned. What's goin' on, Gaucho?" Trent asked.

Muted laughs rose from the normally disciplined men. The relief they all felt was almost palpable. They had their man back. Just as Cal walked up to see Trent, Congressman Zimmer trotted around the bend. Cal looked past his friend and pointed his finger at the politician, "You son of a bitch, I thought I..."

"Whoa, whoa, whoa. Hold up, Cal," Trent said calmly as he held his friend back. "If it weren't for the Congressman, I'd still be locked up in this Japanese dungeon. Lay off, alright?"

Not easily dissuaded, Cal took a step back. He still couldn't shake the feeling that somehow the Congressman was responsible for the setbacks they'd suffered.

Turning away from Zimmer, Cal addressed his men. "Get us the hell out here, Gaucho."

The team leader nodded and guided them out without anyone saying another word.

Chapter 20
Atlanta, Georgia
11:49pm EST, September 17th

TOM JABLONSKI PULLED his rig into the distribution hub. Driving from Las Vegas wasn't hard. He'd made similar trips for years. It didn't hurt that he was getting paid a serious bonus for arriving on schedule. He wished every cross-country trek were as lucrative.

Waving to the security guard, he pulled up to the guard shack. An extra spotlight blazed on and cut through the midnight blackness.

"Paperwork please," asked the tired looking, middle-aged sentry.

The driver handed over the manifest.

The guard reviewed the documentation and checked his computer to see which terminal to direct the driver to. "Head over to Thirty Seven. Honk once or twice for the loading guys," the man instructed. The bored security guard handed back the paperwork and waved the semi through.

Jablonski was familiar with the routine. He'd been to the hub earlier in the month. Pulling into Terminal 37, he honked twice. He knew from experience that the loading crew would take a minute. Working the graveyard shift meant napping when you could.

After a couple of minutes, three men made a slow exit from the terminal building. Two headed for forklifts and one headed to the truck.

Jablonski hopped out of the cab and handed off his paperwork. After a second to review, the foreman with sleep in his left eye looked up.

"Says you got some electronics set for priority shippin'." Jablonski couldn't tell from the southern drawl whether it was a question or a statement. Better to be nice and get out of here quickly.

"Yeah. I think they're cell phones."

Surprisingly, that perked the foreman's interest. "Hey, they aren't those new smart phones everyone's waiting in lines for, are they?"

"I don't know, man. They just tell me where to take 'em," Jablonski replied.

"You mind if I take a look? My kid's been buggin' me about getting her one of those damned things. I ain't gonna shell out four hundred bucks for one though!" the man flashed the driver a dirty grin.

Jablonski had seen this same routine countless times. *Oops a pallet fell off the truck and a couple pieces fell out.* But Tom was an honest driver. He'd never stolen from his shipments and once scolded his own son when he'd suggested doing so.

"Hey, man, you think we can just get these things unloaded so I can go? It's been a long haul."

The foreman looked at the truck and finally nodded. "If you can get the back unlocked, I'll have my boys get 'er done in a half hour."

Tom Jablonski thanked the man and headed to the back of the trailer. Another hour and he'd be in bed, counting his cash bonus.

Chapter 21
Las Vegas, Nevada
11:03pm, September 17th

THE SSI OPERATORS MADE it back to the Bellagio without incident. Along the way Trent and Zimmer relayed the entire story of their capture and the arena battle. Cal wouldn't admit it, but he was surprised by the Congressman's decision to go back for Trent. It would've been really easy for him to get in the car with Ishi and head back to Vegas. Instead, he'd returned to the lion's den and saved Cal some precious time.

Cal, Brian, Neil, Trent and Zimmer were all comfortably seated in Patel's suite. MSgt Trent looked refreshed after a hot shower and highball of Famous Grouse. He continued his story. "I'll tell you what, Cal, these are some sick fuckers. Who the hell does that kinda shit anymore?"

Cal sipped his drink and pondered the same thing. What had they stumbled on? Underground fights to the death, women for hire, a blackmailed politician; the whole thing sounded too farfetched to be true. He still had more questions for Zimmer.

"Congressman, did you recognize any of the men you met?"

Zimmer shook his head. "They never gave me any names. I'm thinking these guys may be more behind the scenes."

"Any other impressions?"

The Congressman took a sip of his drink and let the question sink in for a second. "I'm not gonna lie to you. Most of the time, I was scared shitless. I got the feeling that I was some kind of pet to them. They looked at me like...I don't know how to describe it. They were looking down at me. It felt like..."

"You were less than nothing," Trent completed.

"Yes. Talk about xenophobic. These guys stick with their own kind," Zimmer finished, still wondering where everything was headed.

Cal stood up and walked to the window. "From here on out, the Congressman stays with us."

"But what about Nakamura's instructions?" Zimmer asked on the verge of panic. He could only imagine what would hit the media without his cooperation. The bloody videos would quickly destroy his life.

"Do you really want to go back with those guys?" Cal asked almost angrily. "My job was to find out who these guys are and to keep you safe. I can't do that unless you stay here. For now, we need to take the chance. Maybe we call their bluff. I have a feeling that you're an important part of their plan. I don't think they'll jump the gun."

"How do you know that?" Zimmer blurted. "How do you know they won't take those videos and plaster them all over the Internet?"

"I don't, Congressman. It's called a calculated risk. Besides, it'll all be a moot point soon."

"Why is that?"

"Because we're gonna take these motherfuckers down."

+ + +

After some further planning, the team dispersed to their new rooms. They were all exhausted and they'd have an early morning wakeup call to start executing Cal's plan.

In all the commotion, Cal had completely forgotten to call Daniel Briggs. Despite the late hour, he figured the sniper might still be awake. He swirled the last remnants of his drink as the phone rang on the other end.

"Cal?"

"Hey, man. Sorry I didn't call earlier."

"Everything okay?"

"I wouldn't really say that, but they're better than they were a few hours ago."

"Anything I can help with?" Daniel offered.

"I don't know, man. Tell you what, why don't you come by my hotel room at eight tomorrow morning. By then we'll be done with our meetings and I might have some questions about Vegas that I'll need some insight on."

"No problem. I'll be there fifteen to eight."

Cal chuckled. "Once a Marine..."

"Always a Marine," finished Briggs. "Every gunny I ever had told me that being on-time was being late."

"Me too, Brother."

Cal relayed the hotel and room number and they said their goodbyes. *What the hell am I gonna to do with the scruffy sniper?*

Next, he placed a call to President Waller. The man was still awake and requested they conference in the other members of the Council of Patriots. After five minutes, everyone was on the line and Cal gave a rundown of everything that had happened.

"How soon until Neil gets all the way into Ichiban's network, Cal?" Waller asked.

"I'm not sure, sir. He's having some trouble because of the level of sophistication."

"Any thoughts on what they're after?" asked President Kelton.

"None yet, sir," answered Stokes. "I'm not getting a good feeling about the convention though. Is there any way we can get it postponed until we know more?"

Waller answered first, "Can't do it, Cal. As much as I hate to put so many people at risk, we don't know if that's their endgame yet. Just make sure you keep us in the loop and we'll alert the authorities if needed."

There were a couple more questions from the Council, but nothing was really resolved. They were all anxiously waiting to see where the investigation would lead. They'd learned to be patient men during their time in office. It was a trait that Cal didn't have. The Marine in him wanted to take out the enemy...now.

Chapter 22
Las Vegas, Nevada
6:47am, September 18th

AFTER A COUPLE HOURS of sleep, the SSI team met over a mound of room service food. Cal had reluctantly allowed Zimmer in on the meeting. In for a penny, in for a pound.

"Neil, please tell me you have SOMETHING we can work with," Cal mumbled through a bite of chocolate croissant.

Neil looked like he'd been without sleep for a week. His usually impeccable dress was marred with countless wrinkles and more than one food stain. It wasn't like the computer geek to go this long without cracking into a system.

Patel yawned and waved away a coffee refill offered by Brian. "Okay. So like we talked about before, Ichiban Gaming's main source of legitimate income is from consulting. Early this morning, I finally got past their last firewall. You wouldn't believe how far these guys reach. They've got contacts all over the world."

"Anything we can use?" asked Trent.

"I'm not sure. What I can tell you is that in recent months they've consolidated a lot of their assets. At first glance it looks almost random, but these guys are pretty methodical. They've divested the majority of their American stock and now own a huge portfolio of real estate and commodities like gold and silver."

Zimmer chimed in. "That's nothing new, is it? Haven't the Japanese had a huge interest in our economy since the eighties?"

"Yes, but this is one entity. I'm also seeing a lot of dead ends. They're reporting internal expenditures that are getting spread across hundreds of banks around the globe. A hundred grand here, a few million there... Since they're a private company, they don't have to make this stuff public."

"Can you see where the money's going?" Cal asked.

"Of course, but it would take me weeks to track the end accounts. Most likely they're wired to an initial banking center then routed again multiple times. It's a real maze. I wouldn't be surprised if they had some internal system for tracking their stuff. There's no way I can access that unless I'm inside their server room."

"How hard would it be to get inside that room?" Cal's mind was already running with possibilities.

"Almost impossible," Neil said matter-of-factly. "Besides, I'm sure they probably have some kind of kill switch to destroy all the evidence in case of an investigation."

"Either way, I think we need to try. Any other ideas?" Cal looked around the group. No one could think of anything better. It was a classic dilemma. They had one of the smartest computer geniuses on the planet, plus nearly unlimited technology at their disposal, but what they really needed was boots on the ground. The CIA was learning the same lesson the hard way. Human Intelligence (HUMINT) was invaluable.

"Let's let this sink in for a couple hours. Meet back here at noon. Don't worry, lunch is on me," Cal deadpanned. It was already after 7:30am and he wanted to make a quick call before meeting with Daniel. He excused himself and headed to his new room across the hall.

He dialed a number and entered the bedroom as he waited for someone to pickup.

"Andrews."

"Andy, it's Cal." Capt. Bartholemew Andrews was Cal's former platoon commander from the fleet. They'd seen a lot of combat together and each had a Navy Cross and wounds to prove it. When they were SSgt Stokes and 1stLt Andrews they had grown close after saving each other from the clutches of death, on more than one occasion. No one ever called Capt. Andrews by his given name. He'd always gone by Andy to his friends.

"Hey, Cal! What's going on?"

The last time they'd been together was during Jessica's funeral. Being assigned to the Marine Silent Drill Team kept Andy pretty busy.

"They still have you serving canapés for the Commandant?" The Marine Silent Drill Team was stationed at Eighth and I, the traditional home of the Marine Commandant. Extra duties for assigned officers often included attending cocktail parties with visiting VIPs.

"All that crap stopped as soon as I went to Silent Drill. Where are you calling from?" Andy was one of the very few people outside of SSI that actually knew what the company did behind the scenes. He'd even been a part of the extract team that had infiltrated Dante West's tunnel system and rescued Cal a year ago.

"Me and a couple of the boys are in Vegas doing some work."

"No shit!? We're heading out there tomorrow for the big convention."

"Which one?"

"The Democratic National Convention."

"Really? I thought you guys just traveled to do shows at football games."

"Usually we do. Apparently, the President pulled a few strings and might've threatened to end a couple careers. He wants to look really presidential for his re-election." Andy's disgust was obvious.

"Maybe we can get together. You think you'll have time?"

"You kidding? We always make time to get out when we're on the road. It's one of the few perks we have."

"That's great. Hey, I was wondering if you could do me a favor?"

"You want me to get a signed picture of Chesty for you?" Andy laughed. Chesty was the name given to the Marine Corps mascot, an English bulldog. The name was a tribute to a Marine Corps legend, Gen. Lewis "Chesty" Puller. Every young Marine learned about Chesty in their first days of boot camp.

"Very funny. No, I was wondering if you could look somebody up for me."

One of the advantages of being near Headquarters Marine Corps was the ability to access information about almost any Marine.

"You actually caught me about to log-off of my work computer. Who do you want me to look up?"

Cal gave him Daniel's name and told him that Briggs was a scout sniper. Using his name and Military Occupational Specialty (MOS), the corresponding record popped up after a couple of clicks.

"Got it. What do you want to know?"

"Just wondering what his current status is. Guy told me he got out with PTSD. Wanted to get a better feel for him."

Cal waited as the Marine Captain scrolled through the record.

"Did multiple tours overseas. Wow. He's got over a hundred confirmed kills. Where'd you meet this guy?"

"I'll tell you when you get out here. What else does it say?"

"Honorable discharge as a sergeant, and...wait a minute," Andy clicked on a note under the Awards section. "Holy shit."

"What?" Cal asked, thinking the worst.

"He's nominated for the Medal of Honor."

"Really?! For what?"

Andy skimmed through the citation and read the highlights to Cal. It sounded like the story Briggs had told him. He'd failed to mention that in the firefight he'd probably killed close to fifty insurgents. What was even more impressive was that it was the SEAL Team Commander that put Briggs in for the nation's highest military award.

An additional note added that the sniper's fire was verified by a UAV that had loitered long enough on station to get video of the entire gun battle.

"Thanks for checking on that, Andy."

"No problem. You need anything else?"

"Nope. Just give me a call when you get in."

"Will do."

Cal placed his phone on the wet bar. *What the hell am I going to do with this guy?*

+ + +

Daniel Briggs knocked on Cal's door precisely at quarter 'til eight. Cal opened it and invited Briggs inside.

"Can I get you anything?"

"No, thanks."

"Any more interesting nights on the street?"

"Not yet."

"I wish I could say the same."

Briggs cocked his head in concern. "Anything I can help with?"

"I'm not sure." Cal didn't know how much he should tell Briggs. On one hand, he knew he probably wouldn't say anything. Most Marines knew how to keep their mouths shut. On the other hand, SSI's mission in Las Vegas was completely off the reservation. If anyone so much as caught a whiff of what they were doing, it could spell real trouble for Cal and the company.

"Do you mind if I ask you a couple questions first?"

"Sure." Briggs nodded.

"Okay. First, anything I tell you today you can consider Top Secret. Cool?"

"Cool."

"Second, what's the deal with the CMH?" CMH is short for Congressional Medal of Honor.

Daniel's eyes went cold. "How did you find out about that?"

"I have ways of finding out anything I need to. You okay with that?"

"Why were you checking up on me?" Briggs accused.

"Wouldn't you do the same thing? You meet this guy that looks like he just stepped out of the jungle and he saves your life. Oh, AND he's a Marine?"

Daniel's temper cooled and he actually laughed. "You're right. I guess I forget how I come across sometimes."

"If it makes you feel any better, I don't like to go into many relationships blind. With the resources I have at my disposal, I usually checkup on everybody I can. So you want to tell me about the CMH?"

After a brief hesitation, Briggs explained. "Apparently the SEAL Commander put me in for it. I don't want it."

"Why not?"

"The damned thing makes it sound like I'm a fucking hero. I'm not. A hero would've saved those guys." Cal could see tears coming to his eyes.

"It's just recording what you did, Daniel. From what it sounds like, you deserve it. And that's coming from a guy who knows a thing or two about awards Marines don't want."

Daniel looked. "What do you mean?"

"Let's just say I won an award for killing some bad guys and saving some buddies. I'd give it away if it meant getting my Marines back. It took me a long time to acknowledge the fact that I did something heroic. I don't think I'm a hero either. I did just what they trained me to do: kill the enemy and take care of my Marines. The faster you come to that realization, the faster you'll heal, man."

Briggs nodded thoughtfully. Was this the missing piece? Was God finally answering his prayers?

Cal went on. "I want to introduce you to some of my guys. We're all part of a company called Stokes Security International; SSI for short. My dad started it a few years back after he got out of the Corps. Who knows, maybe you'll like it enough to stick around. We can never have enough lead-slingers around."

Cal smiled and was pleased when Daniel did the same. He was on unfamiliar ground. Of course he had the authority to hire new employees, but he hadn't yet. Cal just got the feeling that there was something to Briggs that could really complement his team.

He gave Briggs a quick rundown of what SSI did but decided to leave out the covert aspect. Better safe than sorry for now. They talked for a few more minutes. Cal was impressed with Daniel's knowledge of Las Vegas. Like a true sniper, he'd evaluated the area with a cunning eye.

Cal gave his new friend a quick brief on what they were up against. He left out the details concerning Zimmer's blackmailing, and kept it to the threat coming from Ichiban.

"How about you join us for lunch at noon? I can introduce you to the rest of the guys and maybe you can poke holes in our plan."

Daniel accepted the invitation and excused himself to run a few errands.

Cal watched him go, all the time wondering if he'd just found a diamond in the rough.

Ishi had spent the morning trying to run damage control. His father had flown into a murderous rage at the news of the escape. It was only the impending coup that had finally calmed the incensed Nakamura.

"From now on, you will not leave Matsura's sight!" Kazuo Nakamura pointed at the third man in the room. The small man smiled and bowed to his master.

"Matsura has already coordinated our deliveries. It is now a simple matter for him to monitor the situation. I have talked to our contact about recent events. He assures me that he can provide information that will eliminate the threat of this Calvin Stokes."

"What kind of information, father?"

Nakamura glared at his son. "It will be provided to Matsura when I receive it."

"What about the Congressman?" Ishi dared to ask.

Father smiled at son. "I have taken care of Congressman Zimmer. He is no longer your concern."

He walked away. It was a dismissal.

Ishi's embarrassment was complete. His failures laid bare, the young Japanese felt afraid. Would his father keep him from the coming glory? Just as he had the thought, he shook it off. His father wouldn't throw him to the side. Ishi was his only child. Since the day of his birth, they'd groomed him for this moment. Ishi would listen to his father for the time being. Soon enough, he would exact his vengeance on his family's enemies. His father would come to see that all his training was not in vain.

+ + +

The SSI team met at noon. There were no immediate updates from Neil. Cal was desperate for more intel on the Ichiban organization, so he allowed Neil to keep clicking away while the rest of the group talked.

He'd started the meeting by quickly introducing Briggs to his team. It was clear that Zimmer wasn't happy about having an outsider involved, but he wisely kept his mouth shut. After hearing the story about Briggs coming to Cal and Brian's aid, the Congressman couldn't disagree that the sniper might be a valuable asset.

"So now that we have a lock on where Ichiban houses its main servers, we need to get in there and see what we can find. As of now, we don't have anything concrete on these guys. At least nothing we can take to the Feds," explained Cal. "We know they've augmented their own security staff with some Russian thugs. Me, Brian, and Top are compromised. We won't be able to set foot in any of their hotels. That means it'll be up to Gaucho's guys."

Gaucho raised his hand. "How much money are you gonna give us to hit the tables, boss?"

The assembled men all laughed. Leave it to Gaucho to keep it light.

"I'm not giving you a fucking penny, Gaucho," Cal joked. "I heard about your shitty luck in Tunica."

Everyone laughed again. The Hispanic commando did like to spend his time off at the Mississippi casinos. Contrary to what Cal said, he often came home with pockets bulging.

Briggs raised his hand and the room went silent. Up to that point, he'd said little more than hello to the elite team. They all sensed a warrior in him, even without knowing about his exploits.

Cal pointed at him. "Whatcha got, Daniel?"

"I was wondering if maybe I could be one of the guys going into that hotel."

Everyone looked to Cal. It's not what he'd expected. "I really just brought you here for a little Vegas insight. I'm not sure I feel comfortable putting you in harm's way."

"I'll stay out of the way. It's just that I know these places a lot better than these guys. No offense, fellas." He looked around the room to nods of agreement.

"Okay," Cal assented, "Gaucho, use Daniel however you need. I'd prefer he sticks to recon."

Gaucho nodded and patted Daniel on the back.

"Okay, any other questions?" Cal asked his men.

"You want me to stay with the Congressman?" Trent asked.

"Yeah. Make sure that we…"

"Oh shit." Everyone turned toward Neil. He was clicking his mouse frantically, pulling up multiple screens.

"What is it, Neil?" asked a concerned Cal.

"They just posted the murder scene video on YouTube."

Congressman Brandon Zimmer paled and looked close to vomiting.

"I guess they just called our bluff," Cal offered conversationally.

+ + +

After Daniel and the contingency team left, the remaining men crowded around Neil's computer screen. The video was exactly one minute long. There was no sound, only a flickering subtitle: *"Woman butchered by popular politician. More details coming soon."* Zimmer cringed as Beth's naked body flashed into focus. Luckily they'd decided to blur her face, for now. The camera panned around the dismembered body and bloody bed. No one said a word.

I can't imagine waking up to that, Cal thought. Although he'd resisted it before, he now allowed a shred of sympathy for the Congressman's predicament. Cal was pretty sure the man standing next to him had not been the culprit of the gory scene replaying over and over again on the computer screen.

+ + +

"Did you really think that was necessary?" the politician asked Kazuo Nakamura.

"The Congressman forced our hand. He was given explicit instructions. He decided not to follow them. Now he will know that we are very serious about exposing him." Nakamura took another sip of his green tea. Posting the video had been a gamble, especially in the presence of his current guest, but he had to maintain his position of power.

"Very well. How is the rest of our little agreement progressing?" asked the politician, between sips of his own tea.

"The upcoming convention is proving to be a problem."

"Why is that?"

"The Secret Service is being extremely diligent. We are concerned that all the pieces will not be in place on time."

"You assured me that this would not be a problem. What do we need to do to remedy the situation?" the politician asked through gritted teeth. He'd put a lot of faith in the Japanese businessman. They were too far along to turn back. Besides, he'd waited long enough for his day in the national spotlight. Only yesterday, he'd listened as the blithering idiot in the White House had bowed to yet another foreign dictator. The President had become a foreign policy nightmare. It was time for strength within the Democratic Party once more. *FDR must be rolling in his grave,* the politician thought, not for the first time.

"I think we can handle the Secret Service. I am, however, concerned with this SSI organization. Do you have the information you promised?"

The politician smiled. He'd called in a lot of favors for the contents in the manila envelope. There'd also been some substantial bribes to loosen the tongues of some ultra-patriotic federal agents. Nevertheless, the information contained in the envelope would not only take care of the SSI problem, but would bolster the politician's new platform as President. Yes, it was time to clean the skeletons out of the closet. America would be a shining example of strength and transparency. No more pansy pandering to terrorists and third world countries. It was about time America had a real democratic leader at the helm.

"Everything you need is in this envelope. Do not release the information to the public until the hour we discussed. You may, however, use the information to dissuade SSI from further involvement near our little operation."

Nakamura finally smiled to his guest. He would have to remember how ruthless this man could be. Unconcerned, Nakamura knew he had enough evidence to condemn the man should the politician decide to cast the Japanese aside. Besides, the packages that were presently being delivered were his organization's ultimate insurance policy. The two men were connected for better or worse.

+ + +

The Council members sat in stunned silence as the YouTube video replayed across their screens for the second time. Pres. Waller pressed STOP and addressed the group via video conference.

"So as you can see, the ante's just been upped. I'll be heading out to Las Vegas soon for the convention. I'm planning on having regular contact with Stokes. Once I know more I'll get you an update."

The members of The Council of Patriots disconnected from the call. To a man, no one would correctly predict the final outcome of the coming drama.

Chapter 23
Las Vegas, Nevada
9:12am, September 18th

THE DEMOCRATIC PARTY was converging on Las Vegas. The convention began in two days. Congressman Zimmer had already gotten ten phone calls from staffers and fellow Congressmen traveling to Vegas. They all wanted to ask if he'd watched the YouTube video and see if he had a guess as to who the murderer might be. He'd laughed off the questions and asked whether they were the guilty party.

He dreaded every call. His paranoid mind kept telling him that they knew it was him. Zimmer knew they didn't, but he wondered what they'd say when they found out he was involved. They'd crucify him. He didn't think badly of them for it. He knew he would've done the same thing a few months ago. They were as clueless as he'd been.

Zimmer remembered watching all those documentaries about Americans spying for Russia during the Cold War. He wondered how many of those spies were just normal people being blackmailed into betraying their country.

His phone buzzed again. It was his father.

"Hey, Dad."

"I assume you've seen the video?"

Brandon cringed. "Yeah."

"So what are our friends doing about it?"

"They're looking into it, Dad."

"We need to meet, Brandon. Where are you staying?"

Brandon told him. "I'll be there in thirty minutes."

Congressman Zimmer looked down at his phone. The last thing he needed right now was an ass-chewing by good ol' dad. Zimmer walked to the wet bar, poured himself two fingers of bourbon, and drained the glass.

He walked back to his laptop and watched the crime scene video for the twentieth time. It was already up to just over one million views.

+++

Thirty minutes later, Senator Zimmer walked into Brandon's hotel room. He was handsomely attired in the latest golf wear.

"I've only got twenty minutes, Brandon. I'm meeting some colleagues at the Wynn for eighteen, so give me the rundown quickly."

Brandon summarized the events of the past forty-eight hours. Once again, his father didn't interrupt. Brandon knew his father. He'd already be formulating a contingency plan in his head. One of the reasons Senator Zimmer was such a long-standing politician was his ability to think five steps ahead and outmaneuver his opponents. The last true electoral test he'd had was fifteen years earlier when a grandson of JFK decided to try his hand at politics. Voters longed for the dynasty of the past, but the Zimmer machine soon killed the young man's chances. Past dalliances were unearthed and witnesses were paraded onto every morning show on Massachusetts radio and television.

No one could trace the attack back to the Zimmer camp, but they all knew. Mess with the crafty Senator and he'd make your life hell.

Richard Zimmer had mellowed a bit with age. He was comfortable in his position. He'd brokered deals for billions of dollars of government aid and contracts to be funneled to his home state. The voters loved him.

"What does Mr. Stokes have in mind for fixing this problem?"

"Dad, I want to say something, but I think it'll piss you off."

"Out with it, Brandon," growled an increasingly impatient Sen. Zimmer.

"I'm considering turning myself in. I think Cal and his team have done what we asked. I don't feel comfortable putting them in any more danger."

Visibly surprised by his son's request, the Senator took a moment to respond.

"I appreciate you trying to take responsibility for the situation, Son. It seems as though you've grown a bit this week. That being said, I do not think this is the right moment to go to the authorities. I've already privately consulted our attorney and he seems to think that the evidence wouldn't hold up in court. However, in the court of public opinion you would be crucified. I think that's the risk we need to take. With the Presidential election so close, we need to be careful."

Brandon wasn't sure if he agreed with his father. And yet, he was a little relieved to hear that should the worst happen he might not go to jail.

"So what should we do?"

"Let's see what Cal's team comes up with. Maybe they'll get lucky and get their hands on the evidence. Until we give them a shot, let's sit tight and wait."

Once again, Brandon couldn't really argue with his father. The only thing worse than the video was the waiting.

+ + +

Daniel left the hotel and headed to a nearby storage facility. Walking up to the glassed entrance, he typed his personal entry code. Briggs went almost to the end of the straight hallway. His unit was the second to last on the left.

He pulled out his key and unlocked the rolling door, sliding it up. Daniel quickly entered the eight by ten unit and closed the door behind him. He'd rigged a custom lock inside the unit so he could stay undisturbed. After locking the door he turned around and surveyed his unit. Everything was neatly stacked. Just after getting to Las Vegas, he purchased several large metal storage containers. They were each about two feet tall by two feet wide and stretched four feet in length. The damn things were heavy as hell, but sturdy and impregnable by all but the best thieves.

Briggs unlocked the box on the far left and opened the lid. He had a variety of weapons neatly arrayed in mini racks. Since moving to Las Vegas, he'd methodically stocked his private armory. Once or twice a week, he visited a different outdoor store. Occasionally, when he had enough cash, he'd head to a gun shop and pickup a new firearm. Briggs never bought in the same place twice.

The box he examined contained mostly smaller weapons. Other containers held his long rifles. He wouldn't need those, for the time being.

Daniel unslung the backpack from his shoulder and set it on the ground. He picked out a couple of things he thought he might need in the next few days. His sixth sense started to prickle again. He could feel the coming tension. It was the same feeling he used to get before going on a particularly dangerous op.

Although Cal made the current action sound routine, Daniel thought otherwise. There was a storm brewing and the Marine in him wanted to be in the middle of it. Standing in the hotel with Cal and his compatriots, Daniel started to feel at home.

The last time he'd felt this comfortable was when he'd finally won the respect of the acting platoon sergeant of his first scout sniper platoon; a crusty old Gunny who looked like he'd been in the Corps since the days of General Lejeune. The man was a career Marine and respected by every enlisted Marine (and the smartest officers) in the battalion. His most commonly used words were 'shit' and 'fuck'. Like any good Gunnery Sergeant, he was a hard man to please. If you ever expected a compliment from the Gunny, you'd be waiting until the second coming of Jesus.

They'd just completed a grueling training evolution at Twenty Nine Palms. It was the lead-up to Daniel's first combat deployment. He'd shot like a pro all week. In addition, his infiltration into the simulated enemy's camp, the subsequent mock killing of their entire battalion staff, and his successful extraction, earned the platoon outstanding marks from the training officials. The Commanding General had even taken a turn commending the brave sniper team.

The old Gunny had turned to Daniel after the final debrief and imparted some of the sweetest words Daniel would ever hear in the Marine Corps: "Well, Briggs, looks like you're not the shitbag that I thought you were. Now go pack your shit. You're a fucking sniper now."

Briggs remembered the crusty old bird fondly. They'd become as close to friends as the Gunny would allow. Tragically, the brave Marine died early into their second tour in Afghanistan. He died a hero, standing in the open, calling in close air support to destroy a heavily manned enemy position while his lifeblood flowed freely from his right arm that was no longer there.

As he did whenever remembering the man, Daniel said a silent prayer for the old warrior. He knew Gunny was up in heaven giving Jesus a run for his money.

He grabbed another couple pieces of survival gear from a separate box and locked everything back up.

Leaving the storage facility, Daniel Briggs walked with a steadier step. He was a man on a mission. He was a man going home.

Chapter 24
Memphis, Tennessee
9:15am, September 18th

THE FEDEX EMPLOYEE almost laughed out loud as he read the order form. Some businesses just didn't know how to ship merchandise. Take this one, for example. They'd literally paid double to have their packages delivered by 11am. They could've saved half if the same delivery was scheduled for two hours later. *Stupid*, thought the delivery supervisor.

He processed the shipment and scheduled the smaller parcels for local carriers. They'd be gone in under an hour. FedEx knew how to get stuff in and out, fast.

Chapter 25
Eighth & I, Washington, D.C.
9:22am, September 18th

"EVERYTHING READY TO GO, First Sergeant?" Capt. Andrews asked his senior enlisted Marine.

"Yes, sir. Second platoon is waiting by the gate."

"Good. How about we head that way?"

Both Marines, attired in civilian clothing, stepped off toward the company van. They were booked on a commercial flight with the rest of their platoon. Leaving from Reagan National would be easy. In about seven hours, they'd be unloading their gear in Sin City.

+ + +

The White House

"Mr. President, I've got your itinerary for the convention."

The tall president reached for the printed sheet.

"I thought you were gonna start sending these to me on my iPad, Bobby," the President teased his junior aide.

Bobby Johansen flushed in embarrassment. It was true. He had promised to "stop killing trees" as the President liked to say. Unfortunately, being swamped with the planning for the trip to Las Vegas, Johansen forgot to deliver the itinerary electronically. It hadn't helped that he'd gotten an email from that Asian guy when he arrived at the office. Something about a delivery coming in later today. He wished he'd never gotten in that mess during the campaign stop in Columbus. Now he had his unlikely savior asking random questions about the President's toys. The President loved new technology. He was known to spend hours scouring social media sites.

None of the inquiries were incriminating. Hell, Johansen didn't want to lose his job! No, the Japanese guy owned a technology company; something to do with cell phones. He wanted to get the inside scoop on possible upcoming government contracts. It seemed to Johansen that the man wanted to be able to brag to the public once the President received his newest smart phone prior to the official release. The guy seemed nice enough. He had helped Bobby out of that little matter with the Columbus police.

Johansen didn't see the harm. Hell, maybe he could even get a free phone out of the deal.

"So can you send this to my iPad, Bobby?" the President woke Johansen from his thoughts.

"Oh, yes sir. Sorry, sir. I'll send it to you right now."

Chapter 26
Las Vegas, Nevada
9:52am, September 18th

DANIEL HURRIED TO his apartment and rushed to the bathroom. He quickly trimmed his beard and then shaved it off completely. He tied his hair back in a ponytail. Next he took out his one pair of decent jeans and threw on a form-fitting, black t-shirt. He finished the look with a weathered gray sport coat his mother bought him when he'd gone home for his dad's funeral. *I look halfway normal again*, he thought, as he stared into the bathroom mirror. *Mom would like to see me like this.*

He linked up with Gaucho's team twenty minutes later. They were all dressed in varying levels of stylish party attire. No one said anything about his appearance, but he thought he saw Gaucho smile in approval.

Briggs gave the men a quick rundown of the target. They were impressed by the level of detail in his presentation. One of the operators, dressed in an expensive Armani suit, asked Briggs how he knew so much about the place.

"Let's just say I've had a whole lot of time to visit most of the Vegas establishments. Zeitaku's relatively new, so I don't know what your plan is to infiltrate the secure areas."

Gaucho answered the question, "Neil gave us one of his toys."

Daniel didn't have a clue what the man was talking about. He knew Neil was the good-looking Indian guy with glasses. Briggs assumed he was just a computer geek that worked for SSI.

"I don't get it. What toys?"

Gaucho laughed. "Sorry, Compadre. I forgot that you don't really know our man Neil. His dad was some rich Indian dude. He built a big telecom company or something in the nineties. Well, Neil grew up working in his dad's workshop. By the age of ten, the kid could fix or build more shit than his dad's best technicians. So when Colonel Stokes brought Neil to SSI, he put him in charge of the company's R&D shop. You give the guy a problem and he comes up with the solution."

Briggs still looked confused. "Okay. So what about the toy he gave you?"

Gaucho motioned to the dark-haired operator standing next to him. The man handed what looked like an oversized CD case to the team leader. Gaucho pulled out a large disk and held it up. It was about eight inches in diameter and about a third of a centimeter thick.

"This is what Neil came up with for one of our little problems. We kept going on ops where the only way we could see through a door was either to knock it down or use one of those fiber optic cameras."

"What does it do?" Briggs asked.

"You ever see one of those kids toys where you unfold the paper and it turns into a snowflake or something?"

"Yeah, I think so."

"Well, this thing transforms into a ball. Then we can drive the thing on a smart phone loaded with the right software."

"But isn't that pretty obvious if somebody sees it on the other side?"

"I ain't told you the best part. We've been testing a lot of this new camouflage shit. You know, the electronic stuff that makes you look like a chameleon? So anyway, Neil used that technology on The Sphere."

"The Sphere?"

"That's what we call it. Neil came up with some crazy name like Techno-Gyro-Camo-Something. We're all dumb grunts. The Sphere works better for us." Daniel knew they were anything but dumb.

"So this thing can camouflage itself?"

"Yeah. It blends with its background. You can be looking right at it and barely see it. Kinda looks like a mirage. We can also flatten it out with the push of a button. Then it's almost totally invisible. It's not foolproof yet, but it's worked pretty well so far. Saves Bam Bam over there..." he pointed to a large man with bowling ball biceps, "...from having to bash in so many doors."

"So what else can it do?" Daniel was fascinated by the advanced gear. What he would've given to have some of those over in the desert.

"It's got a built-in camera so we can steer it and we can record to the cloud. Neil programmed a couple more features, but we'll save those for later."

"Cool. So where do you want me?"

"I've got you paired with Bam Bam." He turned to the rest of the team. "Let's get a quick comm check before we step off. I don't want my calls to go to voicemail."

The men chuckled and started checking their communication gear. They kept it simple and used cell phones. Most of their communication would be done via text. Only emergencies would be relayed via actual phone calls. They'd picked up the pay-as-you-go phones from a couple local pharmacies earlier.

Daniel checked his new phone and smiled. It felt good to be among warriors again.

+ + +

"Cal, Gaucho just checked in. They're starting to head out," Neil updated the small command group.

Cal looked over at Brian, Willy, and Zimmer. "So to recap, Top, you stay here with Neil and the Congressman. Brian and I will head to the café across the street from the target."

"Why do I have to wear the chick disguise?" complained Brian.

"Neil thought you had the better hips," Cal answered with a grin. "It's better than having to wear this fat suit." Cal patted the belly of his twenty-pound fat suit. There was a prosthetic nose and pair of glasses to go along with the trucker hat he had perched on his head.

"Let's get ready and head that way."

Brian nodded and went into the bathroom to change into his drag outfit. He wasn't happy about it, but he knew that even his mother would never recognize him AND it was much easier to hide weapons under the many layers of his outfit. At least he wouldn't have to wear lipstick.

They walked out of the hotel room five minutes later. Brian walked uncomfortably in his patent leather combat boots. "I swear, if you ever make me do this again, Cal, I'll..."

"Relax, Doc. Next time, we'll get Top to wear the chick getup."

Brian laughed at the absurdity of the mental image. At seven feet tall, there was no way MSgt Trent could pass for a woman.

"If I'm dressing up as the woman, you're paying for dinner."

Cal laughed despite the severity of the situation. They were going into the heart of Indian country. Hopefully, all they'd be doing was observing. The last thing he wanted to do was chase the enemy around Las Vegas in a fat suit.

Chapter 27
Tampa, Florida
11:02am, September 18th

THE YOUNG INTERN MET the mailman at the door.

"Got a couple packages for your office. Here, I'll just put 'em in a box for you. Leave the empty container outside tomorrow."

The staffer took the box and looked down at all the labels. She'd planned on leaving early. She was jumping on a plane tomorrow with the rest of Congressman Unger's staff. The past week seemed a blur of planning and scheduling. Her boss was a second-term member of the House looking to get re-elected. Despite the

President's waning popularity, Unger still wanted to get to Las Vegas early and be in as many photos with the incumbent as possible.

Her daddy, a rich Florida businessman, secured her a position through a couple of well-placed donations. When she'd first started working at the Congressman's office, she'd started a casual relationship with the twice-married Representative. His second wife was on the way out, and the staffer was on the way up.

Three months earlier, Unger off handedly mentioned that she should consider dating other people. He threw out some excuse about the re-election and trying to reconcile with his wife. She'd been offended but took it in stride. If she ever wanted a political career, she needed to have a level head. Besides, the Congressman wasn't fun anymore. He'd almost become a recluse in recent months. In fact, she thought, it all started with that trip out to Las Vegas in May. Strange.

She lugged in the mail and sorted through the junk. Picking up a small package, she inspected the label. *Opel. I'll bet this is that new phone he wanted me to order for him.* The pretty intern walked into the Congressman's vacant office and set the package on his large desk. On second thought, she grabbed a sticky note and wrote *"Let me know if you need help using this"* with a smiley face. It was better to keep all of her options open. Maybe Las Vegas would be a chance to climb back into his bed.

She left the office, already planning on which skimpy lingerie to pack.

Chapter 28
Las Vegas, Nevada
11:11am, September 18th

MINUTES AFTER CAL LEFT to monitor the raid, there was a knock at Neil's door. He was so engrossed with his work that he didn't hear the knock or see the manila envelope slide under the door.

Gaucho's teams had already entered Zeitaku at staggered intervals. Some were in pairs of two, others as threesomes. It would be up to him to penetrate the casino's labyrinth with their little toy. They would only have one chance. It couldn't be wasted.

The team leader found the access door right where Neil had described. He glanced around casually and picked out a couple of his men. They were doing what they did best: blending in. Moving to the door, he rolled his suitcase behind. If anyone asked, he was looking for his room. His luggage was actually full of clothes. Tucked in the side pocket was their little surveillance tool.

Once next to the access point, he stopped and parked his bag. Luckily, there weren't any security guards nearby. There were, however, plenty of cameras. The drop would need to be smooth. Gaucho had just the thing. He'd tucked a map in front of the folded surveillance piece. Unzipping the side pocket of his suitcase, he extracted the map, keeping The Sphere covered right behind.

Staring at the travel guide, he used his peripheral vision to detect any wandering eyes. Nothing. Without taking his eyes off the map, he depressed the small power switch on the covert surveillance unit. He could just barely feel it vibrate as it powered on.

Gaucho waited five seconds more, mumbled a few curses for the sake of the cameras, turned quickly, and "accidentally" dropped the map. It fell perfectly flat, The Sphere safely on the ground. He bent over, still cursing to himself, and picked up the map. As he stood, he placed a perfect kick behind the barely visible disc and it slid under the door.

Taking his time with the map, he finally folded it up and slid it into his pocket. Next, he pulled out his phone and texted *GO* to Cal, Neil, and the rest of the team. He headed to the only place on the main level without cameras: the bathroom.

"He's in," Cal whispered to Brian. They'd been at the little café long enough to have half their coffee.

"So how come we can't control that thing from our hotel?"

Cal took another sip of his coffee, then answered. "The signal won't go that far. We've gotta be pretty close to direct it."

"How long do you think it'll take?"

"As long as Gaucho can keep the thing moving, it'll probably be around twenty minutes. Thirty tops."

"So tell me again how that thing is gonna help us?" Brian asked between glances across the street.

"Neil thinks that if we can get close to their internal servers, he'll be able to tap into them. I think he's using The Sphere to send a signal at close range. Once he does that, Neil says we'll have unlimited access to their entire network."

"I guess we better pray that the batteries don't run out."

Cal snorted and went back to pretending to read something on his cell phone. Soon he should be able to see the feed from the surveillance unit. This thing had to work. He had a feeling the Japanese contingent was planning something big.

+ + +

Gaucho settled into the handicap stall at the end of the bathroom. He propped his suitcase against the door and pulled out his phone. Switching on the display, he brought up the appropriate app. While he waited for it to load, he plugged in a pair of headphones.

The screen changed to a large green button. He pressed it. A few meters away, The Ball ballooned into a sphere. Gaucho could now see through the tiny camera. It was an unremarkable hallway that looked huge from the small camera's perspective.

He texted to Cal and Neil: *YOU GETTING THIS?*

They both replied: *YES.*

Following the small map Neil had drawn, Gaucho guided the silent vehicle to its destination.

+ + +

Neil watched his creation move closer to Ichiban's server room. He wished he could be driving the thing, but Cal had insisted on keeping him at the hotel. He was too valuable to put in harm's way. Neil agreed on some level, but he always ached to be with the guys in the field. Sometimes he went along in a support capacity, but they never let him near the action.

He stood up and did some quick stretches. Once they were in the server room, he'd be busy trying to dissect the network. Might as well get in some exercise.

Ever since arriving at the hotel, he'd averaged two to three hours of sleep per night. In order to stay awake, Neil would occasionally do a couple sets of push-ups or burpees, just to get the blood flowing and jumpstart his brain.

As he lowered himself down to the ground for the first of fifty fast push-ups, he spied the manila envelope at the door. Curious, he stood up, walked to the door, and opened up the envelope.

It contained a simple message: *WE KNOW ABOUT THE COUNCIL*

Neil cursed and ran to his phone.

Cal watched as Gaucho carefully guided the remote vehicle through the winding maze. Two times he'd quickly swerved around walking employees who were oblivious to the spy camera's presence. He almost jumped when his phone buzzed with the incoming call. He looked at the caller ID. *What does Neil want?*

He put the phone to his ear. "What's up?"

"We've got a problem."

"Tell me something I don't know, Neil."

"I just got a message," Patel knew the capabilities of agencies like the NSA. Nothing you said on a cell phone was safe anymore.

"Can't this wait?"

"No. I need you back here right now."

Cal looked at Brian and shrugged. "Okay. I'll be there in ten."

Ramirez looked at his friend. "What's going on?"

"No idea. Apparently, we're in another shitstorm. Neil won't tell me until we get back to his suite."

"You want me to stay here?"

Cal thought about it. On one hand, having an extra pair of eyes might be useful. On the other, Gaucho's boys were more than capable.

"No, come back with me. I might need your help."

Brian waved for the waitress to bring the check while Cal texted Gaucho to let him know he'd be off station. What else could be added to this little adventure?

Ten minutes later, the costumed duo entered Patel's suite. Neil motioned them over to the scattered papers on his makeshift desk. The first thing Cal noticed was the note from the envelope: *WE KNOW ABOUT THE COUNCIL.*

"What the fuck?"

"I told you it was bad. It gets worse though, Cal." Neil pointed at the contents of the mysterious envelope. "I think they're trying to tell us something."

"What are you talking about?"

Neil exhaled. He knew he had to keep his friend calm. "I think they're trying to say that we better leave or they'll expose the Council."

"But there's no way they could know about it, Neil!"

"Well, apparently someone pieced it together. It doesn't look like something you could take to court, but they sure could cause a stink."

"How the hell did this happen?" Cal wondered aloud.

The crooked politician started his investigation into the secret group nearly two years before. It all started as an accident. The aspiring President wasn't new to Washington. Over the years, he'd fought hard to head certain committees and cement important relationships. Very diligent in his planning, the long-serving federal servant knew the importance of building a resumé. He now chaired one of the highly coveted intelligence oversight committees.

On this particular occasion, a certain suspected terrorist cell was tracked to the United States by federal agencies. The problem was that The Patriot Act could only do so much. The President had already given explicit instructions that action would only be taken against suspected terrorist cells at home or abroad if the reviewed intelligence proved that the party was guilty beyond a reasonable doubt. Intelligence is rarely absolute. There isn't always a smoking gun. To make matters worse, cells operating in America had become very skilled at evading authorities and masking their activities.

One of the favored ways these groups stayed out of the reach of the law was to conduct clandestine meetings in mosques. Terrorists knew the American President drew the line at entering these holy places of worship. One of the pillars of his election was to repair the American relationship with the Muslim world. What sounded like a noble goal had turned into an open invitation. Ever since the Presidential inauguration, foreign fighters who'd managed to enter the U.S. flocked to mosques and made them their base of operations.

This particular cell, though new on the intelligence radar, was already very accomplished. Recruitment in the Detroit area increased alarmingly. As one of the hardest hit areas as a result of the recent economic downturn, young Arabs were easy targets.

The politician remembered grilling the FBI representatives that stood before his committee. He couldn't believe they were incapable of doing anything. Their reply was always the same: "Our hands are tied."

He'd thought the agency would somehow get creative. It scared him to think that America's enemies could so easily infiltrate his country. Something must be done.

A week later, he happened to run into former President Hank Waller. The two men were members at the same exclusive country club in Annandale. They'd been acquaintances in the halls of Washington for years. Over martinis, they caught up on each other's lives and commiserated on the trajectory of the American economy. Smoking cigars in the member lounge, the politician broached the subject of terrorists on American soil. Waller's brow furrowed. He could tell something was bothering his old colleague.

The politician proceeded to rail against the current President's asinine policy of treating terrorists like prisoners of war. He went on to describe a laundry list of potentially important operations that never launched just because the President wanted to be careful about offending the international community.

"Damnit, Hank. This man is making us look like a bunch of pussies!"

Waller calmed his friend and asked if there was anything he could do to help. Maybe a friendly meeting with the new President?

"That won't help. He's got his guard of cronies that make sure no one rocks the boat. During the election, he was all about reaching across the aisle; working together to affect change. Now he won't talk to a soul if his staff catches wind that they're trying to push an opposing agenda. The man is playing emperor in his ivory palace!" huffed the tired politician.

He'd continued by describing the case of the suspected terrorist cell in Detroit. "I mean, they are on

OUR soil and we can't lift a finger until they jaywalk or murder someone. It's ludicrous."

Waller hadn't promised anything. He'd simply told him that if he ever needed to vent again, his door was always open. After all, he was retired. Both men laughed and promised to stay in touch.

The politician didn't think about the conversation until two weeks later. FBI reps were set to give his committee an update on the Detroit operation. What he received was far different.

"Sir, just this morning, we found out that the Detroit terror cell has been...well, it's been eradicated," informed the obviously confused FBI agent.

"What do you mean it's been eradicated, Mr. Pratt?" the politician questioned suspiciously.

"Well, sir, the two leaders of the cell and their top lieutenants were found this morning in front of their mosque."

"And...?"

"They were all dead, sir."

The politician sat back and digested the news. Certainly the FBI hadn't had anything to do with it?

"Were we involved, Mr. Pratt?"

"No, sir! In fact, we got the tip into our regional office at five this morning. I think we knew about it before the mosque did," Pratt paused, seemingly trying to formulate his next comment. "There's more, sir."

"More? I can't wait to hear this, Mr. Pratt." The politician rolled his eyes turning to his colleagues.

"This was a warning, sir."

"How so?"

"Each man lying on the ground held a large poster board with a message and a package. I have a picture for you here, sir."

"Why don't you save us some time and read it, Mr. Pratt," the politician recommended impatiently.

"It says 'America welcomes all races and religion. What we don't tolerate is terrorists trying to kill our country and our people'."

The committee sat back in shocked silence. Although quietly rooting for the vigilantes, the politician understood the possible fall-out.

"Thank you, Mr. Pratt. If you'll please leave copies of your documentation we will call on you again soon."

The politician had tried not to rush as he'd taken his assigned packet. It seemed that whoever had murdered the terrorists had first done their homework first. Each man had a nametag stuck to his shirt. They were given names like PEDOPHILE, COWARD, and BLASPHEMER. In each package, they'd included the evidence to explain their nicknames. One man had a DVD showing close to six hours of the dead man having sex with ten-year-old prostitutes. The next man's package contained a thumb drive with hours of audio. Each recorded conversation was the dead man talking with one of his colleagues. They were laughing about the naïve recruits that strapped bombs to their bodies. The man actually said, "I would never be stupid enough to do that. They are so easy to convince in this country."

The transcripts went on and on. These men were obviously guilty. To cap it all off, the killers also provided audio, video, and schematics recovered from the deceased terrorists. The plans detailed an operation soon to be executed. They were targeting public elementary schools. The captured video showed the terrorists casing local educational institutions at the start of the school day. Based on the information provided, the FBI had already raided the terrorist safe house and uncovered crates of automatic weapons, RPGs, and hand grenades.

The politician was impressed by the daring killers. Whoever had conducted the investigation and the subsequent killings were professionals. Someone was secretly doing things right.

Over the next week, more and more intel was mined from the contents of the Detroit safe house. No one cried for the loss of these men. Surprisingly, once the truth of the dead terrorists' background and operation leaked to the press, the local Muslim community understood and calmed. They knew it was a warning to other would-be terrorists and not a threat to them.

The politician marveled at the effect of the killings. While listening to the testimony of countless FBI representatives, he started to wonder how the initial investigation leaked to the covert masterminds.

During one particularly boring hearing, the conversation with President Waller popped into his head. *Could it be? Is that the leak?* At first, the politician chided himself for his indiscretion. A plan formulated in his mind. Maybe if he let another piece of actionable intelligence slip to Waller, the problem would take care of itself.

The politician had found out long ago that in the corridors of Washington's elite, there was no such thing as knowing too many of other people's secrets.

That night, he carefully went over every supposedly dead-end operation he knew about. These would commonly be called 'cold-cases' in a police department. He liked to call them 'grey cases.' They lived in a grey area where either the evidence could only be collected through less than legal tactics or the suspected criminal was untouchable due to the person's station or status under current law.

Federal agencies hadn't 'officially' given up on them, but the mix of current regulation and the sitting President made convictions nearly impossible. After much reflection, the politician knew the perfect case to leak.

The next day, he placed a call to Hank Waller's office. Because of his status in Washington, he was immediately patched through. During the brief chat, the politician never mentioned the Detroit operation. Instead, he invited President Waller to play eighteen holes at the Army-Navy Club the next week.

Waller quickly checked his schedule and confirmed that he could make the tee time.

The following week, the two competitive men, surrounded by a roving Secret Service team, did their best to out-putt and out-drive each other. After the ninth hole, the politician steered the conversation to the increasing problems on the U.S.-Mexico border.

"It's pretty pathetic that the President has his attorney general crucifying these border guards. Did you hear that last week we actually had one of our outposts shelled?"

Waller looked up in surprise. "As in mortar shelled?"

"Yes," the politician knew he had Waller's attention. "The drug cartels are getting their hands on anything they want. What's next, heavy artillery?"

"Why aren't we doing anything about it?"

"These guys aren't idiots, Hank. They sit just on the other side of the border and wage war. We don't cross the border because Mexico is our ally. Problem is, the Mexican authorities are completely overwhelmed. They've got their hands full in major cities where hundreds of people are being murdered in broad daylight. What do they have to gain by helping us protect OUR border? Hell, a lot of their revenue comes from illegal immigrants coming over here and shipping money back to Mexico."

"So why doesn't the President put the screws to Mexico? I know we've done some joint ops before. We can help them if they need the help."

The politician laughed. "Are you kidding? When was the last time you saw the President put the screws to any foreign leader? I think the only country he's had a real pissing contest with is Israel. And they're our allies! No, he doesn't like making waves. He'd rather send drones into Pakistan than bitch slap a neighbor."

"That sounds pretty harsh," Waller scolded.

"It's the truth, Hank. Come on. You've been in the hot seat. You know how it goes. Give these guys an inch and they take a whole country."

The politician went on to tell the ex-President about the powerful cartel that was changing the face of the border war. Led by a secretive gangster, the expanding organization now played gatekeeper for other cartels looking to ship their illegal goods into America. The mortar attack was suspected to be the work of the same cartel.

Waller listened intently. The politician wouldn't know until nearly a month later that Waller had passed the information on to a secret band of warriors.

✦✦✦

This time the results of the clandestine operation came from the DEA representative to the politician's committee. The man described, in detail, the load of intel that had recently been anonymously sent to their office. As a side note, the DEA man reported that the head of the border cartel had recently been found and gagged outside the regional Mexican police headquarters. Attached to the man were ten kilos of cocaine and enough video evidence to incarcerate him and his associates for hundreds of years.

So these covert warriors weren't just killers. They had the ability to deliver criminals alive to the authorities when appropriate.

The politician filed the thought away. He then set about having his contacts get him information on President Waller's conversations and travels. He hadn't known the exact identity of the organization conducting the covert operations, but he would soon.

The highlights of the almost two-year secret investigation filled the space the size of a large manila envelope. It was a pity he'd have to break up the party, but it was for the greater good: America's future.

+ + +

Cal and Brian sifted through the contents of the envelope. There were pictures of Council members together at various locations along with snippets of conversations. It sounded like someone had paraphrased after listening in. Maybe some of their Secret Service Agents?

All the documents felt more like a precursor. They were incomplete. Something was missing. What was it? What were they getting at? They seemed to be saying, "If you think this is a lot, just wait until you see what else we've got."

Maybe it was just a fishing expedition. Maybe whoever 'they' were didn't know anything. They were making one point painfully obvious: by delivering the envelope right to their suite, they knew where they were AND they knew about their connection to the Council of Patriots.

Cal picked up the secure phone next to Neil and dialed a number from memory. It was a number he swore he'd never use. He waited as the secure connection went through.

Hank Waller answered, "Yes?"

"Mr. President, we have a problem."

Chapter 29
Las Vegas, Nevada
12:28pm, September 18th

THE GROUP of Japanese men sat around the conference room table, chatting with colleagues as they waited for their host to begin.

Kazuo Nakamura looked around the room and remembered days long gone. These men truly were like family. Their histories were forever intertwined.

Kazuo's father, Akemi Nakamura, had been close to fifty when his son was born. His first wife, who'd left him childless, died six years earlier. His second wife was twenty-five years his junior. He'd married her simply to produce an heir.

The second wife produced a son, but died from complications during his birth. Young Kazuo was raised by an elderly housekeeper and occasionally allowed to enter his father's world.

At the age of nine, Kazuo awoke late one night. He heard loud shouting from the other side of the house. Being in a traditional Japanese home, most of the doors were literally paper-thin. He crept towards the commotion and peeked through a small hole in one of the door's panes.

He observed his father and four other men sitting around their chabudai dining room table. His father pointed at one of the men across the short table and yelled, "You know how that makes us look! You take advantage of the American contracts, but you will not be social with them!"

The man kept his head bowed in deference and tried to explain. "But, Nakamura-san, these Americans will do more business with us if I find the time to eat dinner with them or..."

"NO! I SAID NO! You must never associate yourself with them outside of business. We will use them for now, but soon Japan will be ours once again. The next time..."

The elder Nakamura stopped in mid-sentence. Even at close to sixty years of age, he was still physically commanding. Not a day passed that Kazuo's father didn't practice in the family dojo. Looking straight at

Kazuo, he sprang up and moved to the door. Young Kazuo knew there was no sense in running. He'd felt his father's wrath before.

The elder Nakamura's hand shot through the thin papered pane, grabbed his son by the back of his head, and threw him into the room. He'd proceeded to methodically beat his son. There would be no cuts or bruises on his face or hands, but his torso would be black and blue for weeks. He was sure that his father had broken at least two ribs in the process.

The next day, his father walked into his room. Kazuo was at his desk doing his homework.

"Come with me," his father ordered.

With a wince, Kazuo rose and followed.

They entered the family dojo and the old man turned to his son. "Have you learned your lesson?"

"Yes, Father."

"Good. The next time you are caught spying..." he let the threat linger as he turned to the small shrine situated in one corner.

He grabbed two sake glasses, filled them, and handed one to his son.

"I have a story to tell you, son. Drink first, then we talk."

Kazuo did as instructed and gulped down the fiery liquid. It was his first taste of sake, but far from his last.

His father produced a pile of papers from a locked compartment under the small shrine. Kazuo looked at him anxiously.

"Have I ever told you the history of our family, My Son?"

"No, Father."

Akemi Nakamura nodded and spread the papers on the floor then knelt. Son followed. The first thing young Kazuo noticed were the pictures of his father. He was always standing in uniform. He knew his father has served in World War II, but he didn't know in what capacity.

"I was very young when I entered my first military academy," his father began. "At that time, we had a very strong force. Because my father was a prominent politician, I was given the choice of where to serve. After excelling in my studies and training, I was selected to serve with our Military Police. We were called the Kempeitai. I was recruited to be part of their elite interrogation unit. I trained extensively with the German Abwehr. Some of my friends flew to Italy to train with the Italian Military Intelligence called the Servizio Informazioni Militare, or SIM. It was a wonderful time in our history. The Empire reached farther than we ever had in our history. I spent much time in China and the Pacific islands. We captured and tortured our enemies. I was a very good interrogator. They called me Akemi. Do you know what that means, my son?"

"I think it means Beauty of Dawn, Father."

"That is correct. Now, what is on our national flag of Japan?"

"A rising sun, Father."

"Yes. I was named Akemi because of my cruelty and success. My fellow soldiers saw my actions as bringing about the new dawn. The rise of the Empire of Japan."

"But, Father, is Akemi not your real name?"

"It is now. That is another part of the story. As I was saying, we conquered wherever we went. Our warriors could not be stopped. The Pacific Islands, China, and Australia were all within our grasp."

Nakamura's eyes clouded. "That all changed with the invasion of Pearl Harbor."

"I thought that was a great victory for our people, Father."

"It was, my son. But it was only one battle. And that small victory awoke the American giant. Yes, we fared well at first. I still remember the newspapers filled with sinking American warships. It was a glorious time to be Japanese. But, after a time, the Americans recovered. Soon they were shipping unlimited resources to the Pacific. Our warriors fought valiantly...but, of course, you know the rest."

Father and son sat silent for a moment. Akemi seemed to be gathering his thoughts again.

"After the war the Americans came looking for war criminals. I knew that what I did was in service of the Emperor. It did not matter to the Americans. They tracked down many of my friends. Most were hung or shot."

Kazuo's eyes went wide with wonder. "What happened to you, Father?"

"I was eventually caught. Luckily, I had forged documents with my new name, Akemi Nakamura. My other stroke of luck was that anyone who witnessed what I'd done was now dead. That is, all except for a few of my men. Some were captured and some escaped. The gentlemen you saw last night were four of them. I was imprisoned until no evidence could be produced to prosecute me. I found a new home and started my new life. Over the years, I found some of my old comrades. Most have new names as well. We meet periodically to reminisce about the old days and talk of the future."

Kazuo stared at his father with awe. His father had been a great warrior of Japan, just like the mighty Samurai he learned about in school.

The next time his father's friends came for a visit, Kazuo was invited. He was always instructed to sit and stay quiet. A trend quickly emerged in Kazuo's mind. They were planning something. What was it?

Soon, with the approval of the elder Nakamura, the other men started bringing their own sons to the gatherings. Kazuo became their leader. Not only did they spend time together at the Nakamura household, they would run in the hills and play Samurai. Little did he know then that gatherings for monthly dinners would one day become what it was today.

He forged those relationships through his teenage years and his father slowly prepared him for the future.

There was always the lesson of putting Japan first. They talked for hours about their ancestors as they trained in the dojo. Kazuo remembered those days fondly.

Then came the day when the military police came to his home. By some cruel twist of fate, the modern day version of the Japanese Kempeitai had found his father's true identity. Enough evidence was presented at the trial to lead to a swift prosecution. The war criminal, Akemi Nakamura, and his associates were killed by a Japanese military firing squad at the age of sixty-eight.

No one thought to question the children.

Kazuo Nakamura assumed leadership of Japanese outcasts. Instead of mourning, he turned his sights on the ultimate goal: returning the Empire of Japan to its former glory. He had two enemies to confront: first, the current Japanese leadership and second, the United States. He saw the two as being the parties guilty of killing his father. He would not forget.

He led a delicate balancing act in the ensuing years. Nakamura pursued his education both in Japan and in the United States. Instead of being outwardly hostile to non-Japanese, Kazuo encouraged his small band to branch out. They learned about their enemies and entrenched themselves in both the Japanese and American political systems.

Nakamura's patriots slowly grew over the years. Now, there were close to twenty men in the inner circle.

The influence of the group extended throughout the Japanese and North American economies. They studied their enemies and gained leverage whenever possible.

Kazuo relocated to America when his son was born and raised Ishi as an American. They'd first lived in San Francisco, then moved east and settled into Wellesley, a quiet suburb of Boston. At the age of nine, his son was indoctrinated into the group. He'd been an apt pupil.

By dumb luck, Nakamura had stumbled upon what would become one of their greatest assets. During Ishi's freshman year of private high school, he'd become friends with the son of a famous celebrity. At first, the strict father had forbidden the relationship. He didn't want his son THAT Americanized.

One of Kazuo's strengths as a businessman was to always search for the silver lining of unintended consequences. For years, he'd tried to figure out how to infiltrate America's capital. So far, he'd only achieved marginal success. His son's high school friendship gave him another idea. What if his son and the children of his compatriots became the friends of prominent politicians? He decided to try an experiment. First, he made discrete inquiries.

The next morning, he instructed Ishi to begin cultivating a relationship with the son of a long-standing U.S. Congressman. The two were in the same private high school but had never mingled in the same groups. Later that day, Ishi returned home to tell his father that the Congressman's son had rebuffed his attempts at friendship.

After a severe rebuke, Kazuo calmed down and gave his son more to work with.

"I want you to do anything you need to. Find out if the boy uses drugs. Maybe he likes girls and alcohol. Observe without being obvious."

Ishi agreed and the next day came home with the expected details.

"Father, I followed the boy and his friends at a discreet distance and found that they do like marijuana. In fact, I saw them smoking behind the football bleachers."

His father smiled. "Good work, my son. We have our way in."

Over the next week, father and son crafted a scheme to get Ishi into the boy's clique. Through his contacts, Kazuo Nakamura purchased medical-grade marijuana. He had Ishi practice smoking the drug in order to understand its effects and to learn how to maintain control. The next week, Ishi joined the boys behind the bleachers.

The Congressman's son, a fat spoiled teenager, confronted Ishi. "We don't want Japs hanging around us."

His friends laughed, but Ishi ignored the comments. Instead, he pulled out a carefully rolled joint, lit it, and took a long hit. The boys' eyes opened wide and menace changed to wonder.

"Where'd you get that, Jap boy?" asked the Congressman's son.

The young Nakamura looked straight into the boy's eyes and pointed at him. "First, my name is Ishi," he paused to take another hit. He could almost see the boys salivating. "Second, you want some?" He motioned to the boy with his joint.

"What is it?"

"It's something special."

"Is it laced with something?"

Ishi shook his head. "Nope. Just some shit stolen from a government lab."

The other boys all looked to the Congressman's son. They knew what his father did. They waited for him to lead.

The boy smiled and grabbed the joint hungrily. "I think you're gonna fit in just fine around here, Ishi."

It was a huge lesson for the Nakamuras. They now understood how their targets could be manipulated. Simply find their vice and exploit it. It was a formula they continued to use. Nakamura instructed his Japanese compatriots to do the same with their children and their businesses. Soon, their results surpassed Nakamura's wildest predictions. Blackmail was a powerful tool.

After doing some research, Kazuo found another interesting weakness he could exploit. The sons of prominent bureaucrats tended to follow in their fathers' footsteps. Over the years this phenomenon created families that would become political dynasties. It was time to attack the governmental elite.

During college, Kazuo Nakamura chose Ishi's target: The Zimmer Dynasty.

The Nakamura's ultimate victory neared. Their blackmail list stretched far and wide. Leading Japanese politicians and businessman, hungry for additional international market share and respect, had privately endorsed Nakamura's bold plan. In exchange for crippling the American machine, they would push through the reform needed to bring Japan back to superpower status. Yes, it would mean some minor disputes in Asia. But the ends justified the means. Besides, they would have the tacit approval of the next American President. The Empire of Japan would rise again.

+ + +

Back in his posh suite, the politician ran the details through his mind. He wished the coup didn't involve the Japanese, but that was now beyond his control. So far, they'd succeeded in their planning. If worse came to worst, he could always point the finger back at them.

Grabbing his gin and tonic, he sat down and prepared for the mayhem.

Chapter 30
Las Vegas, Nevada
1:34pm, September 18th

PRESIDENT WALLER AND CAL decided that meeting to review and discuss the packet was worth the risk. Cal agreed to meet the former President in under an hour.

Meanwhile, Neil had successfully hacked his way into the Ichiban internal servers. He was now downloading the mountain of information for his software to start analyzing. Patel also had a team ready to assist at his office back at SSI headquarters.

Because of the fact that the enemy somehow knew their location, Cal had a dilemma. What they needed to do was move Neil and all his equipment. The problem was that they needed it up and running.

Instead of relocating, Cal instructed Gaucho to pull his troops back to the suite and secure it completely. Barring a cruise missile, the suite would be untouchable.

On a whim, Cal decided to bring Briggs along. The guy knew the city and the best way to navigate it. There was a reason he was a "scout" sniper.

The two Marines set off for the meeting with Waller. Rather than follow the outdoor walkways, Briggs cut a path through the casinos. It was possible to travel through much of The Strip without even stepping outside.

Cal casually swept his gaze as he'd learned in Todd Dunn's challenging counter-surveillance course. He couldn't detect any tails. Daniel pressed on.

The pair finally reached the small room that Neil had just reserved at the Treasure Island Resort and Casino. They wouldn't need it for long, which was good. Waller had come with minimal security and in a casual disguise. Luckily, ex-Presidents weren't highly important targets or his Secret Service staff might have denied the last minute request.

Cal nodded to the large man in jeans standing outside the door.

"Sorry, sir. I was instructed to only let you in," the agent said.

Cal looked at Daniel. "Do you mind waiting out here?"

"Nope. See you in a minute."

Cal opened the door and approached the next agent, who quickly frisked him. He pointed to Cal's wrist that had his knife strapped to it. Just as the agent went to make a comment, Waller came out of the bathroom.

"He's fine, Jimmy. Why don't you wait outside?"

The agent looked like he was about to object, but instead nodded and stepped out.

"So, what are we dealing with here, Cal?"

Cal pulled his backpack off, extracted the manila envelope, and handed it to Waller.

Sitting down at the coffee table, President Waller took out the evidence and spread it out. His left eyebrow arched as he quickly perused the collection.

"Somebody's been doing their homework, haven't they?"

"Yes, sir."

"Do you guys have any idea who might be behind this?"

"I'm new at this whole thing, Mr. President. I don't know who you've had contact with in the past. My concern is that some of your security detail could be the issue."

Waller stared at Cal for a moment. "I really hate to think about that, Cal. How realistic could it be?"

Cal had thought about it on the way over. "The way I see it, Mr. President..."

"Come on, Cal, it's Hank in here, remember?"

"Yes, sir. Sorry, Hank. Anyway, it is possible that someone could have taken these pictures and gotten audio from a long way off. The problem is, how did someone know where to look? I'm assuming whenever the Council meets, the number of people that know the itinerary is minimal?"

Waller nodded.

"Well then, there has to be someone on the inside."

Waller stood up and walked to the window. "You know how bad this pisses me off? It reminds me of all the times Trav warned us about OpSec. He kept telling us that at some point someone would figure things out. How bad do you think this is?"

"I made a secure call to Trav before coming over. They're running some scenarios," answered Cal, unsure of what else the President wanted him to say.

"I want YOUR opinion, Cal. Does this kill us?"

"You really want my opinion?"

"Yes."

"Okay. I figure we have two options: One, pack up, head home, and let the Zimmers deal with their own mess."

"You know that's not what..."

"Hold on, sir. Let me finish."

"Sorry. Go ahead."

"Second, we can find the leak and plug it."

"And how do you propose we do that?"

"It'll be risky, but I think the rat is about to surface. The other thing I wanted to tell you was that we honestly believe there is going to be some kind of attack or demonstration during the Democratic Convention."

Waller's eyes went wide. "What? How is that even possible? I've been to these things for years. I'm sure the Secret Service has buttoned up the city pretty tight."

"A week ago, I would've agreed with you. But after what I've seen here, I'm not so sure. Hell, these guys found us and, more importantly, figured out about the most secretive group outside of the U.S. government. They've got resources and they aren't afraid to use them."

"So, what's the next step? Should we alert the Secret Service?"

Cal knew he was taking a risk, but he had confidence in his team. "I think we should see how it plays out. Let's say we give the Secret Service an anonymous tip that'll hopefully get them even more attentive. Meanwhile, me and my team find these fuckers and take them out."

Waller looked at the young man. If he felt any doubt, he didn't show it. "Travis was right."

"What do you mean?"

"We need more Marines in this world."

Cal and Waller ironed out a few more details. The ex-President would alert the rest of the Council and have them start thinking about potential leaks. Even though he wasn't close to the current President, Waller still had duties to perform for his Party. Over the next couple days, he would be called upon to attend to the Convention. It would keep him busy, but they agreed to stay in close contact.

Daniel and Cal left the meeting room and headed back. Thinking to himself, Cal barely noticed the passing landscape. He grabbed his phone and dialed Neil.

"Yeah."

"Tell me you've got something, Neil."

"You're not gonna believe this shit. They've got..."

"Hold on. Don't say anything on this line. We'll be back in a few minutes."

"Okay. I'll have a brief waiting for you."

Looking down to replace his phone in his pocket, Cal almost ran right into Briggs. Daniel had casually stopped at a slot machine and placed a quarter in the slot.

"What are you...?"

"Don't look up," Daniel interrupted.

Cal did as told and glanced down at the game. "What's going on?" he whispered.

"Looks like those goons found us again. Three o'clock. I saw at least two of 'em. I'll bet there's more," Daniel answered casually.

"How the hell did they find us?"

Briggs answered with a shrug. If he was concerned, he sure as hell didn't show it.

"What's our next move?" Cal asked.

"I've got a Marine buddy that works on the security team here at Treasure Island. Let me call his cell phone and see if he can get those fuckers off our tail."

Daniel continued to feed quarters into the slot machine as he pulled out his phone and dialed a number.

"Hey, Rick. I've got a favor to ask. You working right now?"

"Yeah, man. What's up?"

"You know those Russian goons that work over at Zeitaku?"

"Ivan Drago lookin' motherfuckers?"

"Yeah. They're in your casino right now and they want to put their hands on me and my friend. Anything you can do to help?"

Daniel could hear Rick already moving through the casino. "I'm on it, brother. Where are they?"

Briggs told him where they were and hung up.

"So who was that guy?" Cal asked.

"Rick was a grunt in my first battalion. Helluva squad leader. Saved his ass a couple times."

Cal's respect for the sniper kept growing. He might be a good friend to keep around.

Two minutes later, Cal heard a commotion. He turned to see a group of ten security guards surrounding the hulking Russians.

"I don't know why you bother me. I here to spend money!" the Russian leader bellowed.

"I'm sorry, sir, but we've received complaints that you've been harassing some of our customers," the head guard informed respectfully. "I'll need you to leave at once, sir."

"I no bother no one, jarhead!" the giant snarled. "Maybe I bother you, instead."

Rick, the former Marine, looked around at his nine guards near the three Russians. "You're more than welcome to try, sir, but I'm not so sure about your odds."

The huge man looked around and weighed his options. His instructions were clear: find Cal Stokes and kill him. It had been one of Ichiban's hookers that had spotted Stokes one casino back and alerted the team. The fact that the man was within earshot only angered the thug further.

"You hear from me again soon, jarhead. We go now."

Rick nodded and motioned for the other guards to escort the trio out. As they moved to the exit, he turned around and headed over to Daniel and Cal.

"Hey, brother. How goes it?" he asked, as he shook Daniel's hand.

"Good, man. Hey, I want you to meet a buddy of mine. Rick, this is Cal."

The two men sized each other up, as only Marines can do, and shook hands.

"Thanks for your help," Cal offered.

"Not a problem. I owe Snake Eyes a couple of favors."

"Snake Eyes?" Cal asked curiously.

"It was my call-sign on patrol," Briggs explained. "While I was in Afghanistan, my mom sent me the whole G.I. Joe DVD cartoon collection. Snake Eyes was always my favorite character and some of the other Marines found out about it and the nickname stuck."

Rick laughed. "Yeah. Dude would come back from an op and sit there and watch those fucking cartoons over and over."

Cal joined in the laughter. "I remember those. I guess the name fits for a sniper."

Briggs nodded. "Thanks again for the help, but we've gotta go."

"No problem, man. Stay in touch, okay? By the way, I like the new look!" He pointed at Daniel's ponytail and hairless chin. Briggs smiled and they all said their goodbyes.

"How close are we?" Cal asked his partner as they descended another set of escalators.

"Not far. About five minutes."

They walked out a back service exit and into an alleyway. Neither Marine saw the small Japanese man, requisite tourist camera slung around his neck, casually looking their way.

"He found them, Father," Ishi informed.

"Good."

"What are his orders?"

"Tell him to kill them, quietly."

Ishi texted the command into his phone: *TAKE OUT THE GARBAGE, QUIETLY*

The Japanese assassin read the text and smiled inwardly. It had been too long since he'd used his skills. Kenji Matsura looked completely harmless. Dressed in a pair of old pleated pants, checkered shirt, and thick glasses, Matsura looked like one of a thousand Japanese tourists wandering the streets of Las Vegas.

His deadly abilities were hidden by his almost feminine. Born into a family of warriors, Kenji Matsura was what some might call a modern day ninja. An expert in four types of martial arts, he was also a veteran of the Japanese Defense Force. Most people didn't know much about the Japanese military. This was mainly due to the fact that after World War II part of the peace treaty declared that the Japanese people could no longer field an army. In recent years, the treaty's provisions had relaxed and Japan had even sent troops to help in the Middle East.

Matsura was part of the first unit sent. Unbeknownst to the public, a group of Japanese military officers had formed an ultra-secretive commando unit within the Defense Force: Unit 47. Through his amazing ability and family connections within the military (certain military officers were privy to portions of the plot orchestrated by Nakamura), Kenji Matsura was assigned to Unit 47.

It was in Iraq where Matsura finally utilized his skills. He was given free reign to track down and kill insurgents and suspected terrorists. His results overshadowed his ruthless tactics. Matsura often worked alone and slaughtered whole families. He'd finally been reined in and sent home.

No matter, Matsura thought. He'd been trained by the Army and battle tested in the desert, but it was Kazuo Nakamura who'd become his true master. Like a brilliant general, Nakamura had recognized Matsura's abilities and put them to frequent use. Many former rivals now called the cemetery their home, thanks to Nakamura's scheming and Matsura's death dealing.

He'd been warned about the prowess of Cal Stokes. It didn't bother Matsura one bit. Other great warriors had tried to kill him before. He'd slaughtered them all. It was time to put another notch on his sword.

+ + +

Daniel sensed the approaching danger a split second before it happened. They'd just entered the rear entrance to the pool deck of the Bellagio, music blaring and bumping from the poolside DJ booth, when he grabbed Cal and threw him into the bushes.

The suppressed pistol round grazed Daniel's chest as he spun around for cover. He reached for his concealed pistol as he fell.

+ + +

Matsura couldn't believe he'd missed. He'd had Stokes in his sights, been completely quiet and concealed, yet the man with the blonde ponytail had sensed his presence. The assassin wouldn't make the same mistake again.

+ + +

Cal glanced at Briggs from behind a short wall. Daniel pointed to where the shot came from and he nodded. Why had he not brought his pistol? As if reading his mind, Briggs showed Cal a second pistol. The Marines were about twenty feet apart, but at least they might have a chance of each sporting a weapon. Cal peaked out cautiously and heard a shot fired in response. He quickly whipped back and the bullet hit exactly where his head had just been.

This guy was good. What to do now? Cal texted the team: *ONE MAN SHOTS FIRED BY THE HOTEL POOL SEND HELP*

Hopefully, Gaucho would understand his text.

+ + +

Daniel took a steadying breath and said a quick prayer. He'd been in similar situations before. It almost always came down to decisiveness, daring, and a little bit of luck. Briggs counted down the seconds as he watched the assassin move closer.

Matsura now had two suppressed pistols, one in each hand. He was an expert with both hands. Keeping his weapons pointed at their respective targets, he stalked forward. Two kills in a day was a walk in the park for the warrior.

Gaucho and Neil looked down at their phones at the same time. "Shit!" The room full of operators looked up. "I need four of you right now. Weapons concealed. We're going down to the pool."

The five men sprinted out of the suite, past their surprised sentries, and into the stairwell. Gaucho hoped they'd make it in time.

Briggs made his move, diving out from cover, low to the ground, facing his attacker. There was maybe fifteen feet between the two men. Matsura was faster, his two rounds on a perfect collision course with Daniel's chest as the Marine's double-tap went off a split second too late.

+ + +

Matsura smiled as the bullets hit their target. He felt two stings on his shirt. Had he been shot? Looking down quickly, his eyes squinted in confusion. Instead of seeping blood, he saw two yellow paint splatters.

Just as he turned to find his second target, he realized his folly. The blonde man's dive had been a diversion. He'd sacrificed himself so that Stokes could flank the assassin. The Japanese killer had walked too close. He should have stayed back. During the quick exchange, Cal had taken advantage of Daniel's diversion and crept forward behind the tall privacy bushes.

He sprang up from his squatting position, knife leading the way. The blade went into the assassins left ear to the hilt. The Marine twisted the blade as the man struggled for a moment, and then folded to the ground.

After quickly making sure the man was dead and taking his two suppressed weapons, Cal ran to his fallen friend.

Gaucho's men rushed out onto the pool deck just as the muffled shots went off. The guests looked at them in confusion, most too absorbed in their drinks and the loud music to notice the commotion. The SSI team rushed to the source of the shots.

+ + +

Cal bent down to his new friend. Daniel had signaled what he'd wanted to do, but Cal had shaken his head. This wasn't the sniper's fight. He'd seen the rounds hit. He could only hope that his injuries weren't fatal.

Cal rolled Daniel over and noticed that the wounded man was clutching his stomach. He looked up at Cal. "Did you get him?"

"Yeah. Don't move. We need to get you to the hospital."

"For what?" It was obvious the sniper was trying to catch his breath. They had to get him out of there soon.

"You got shot, man. Don't move. My guys should be here in a second."

As if on cue, the five team members spotted them and hopped over the fence. Gaucho reached the pair first. "He shot?"

Cal nodded. He then pointed to the Asian assassin. "We need to get that body out of here. Can your boys take care of it?"

Gaucho nodded and barked quick orders over the booming music.

Cal started peeling off Daniel's shirt so he could find the entry wounds. When he did one of the bullets rolled off of the sniper's Kevlar covered chest. Cal looked down in confusion.

Daniel gasped as he explained. "I was trying...to...tell you. It just hurts...like a...sonofabitch."

"You lucky fucker," laughed the short Hispanic, shaking his head.

"Wait," Cal stopped, "I didn't hear your pistol shots go off."

Daniel smiled. "These are...paintball...guns." He handed one to his friend.

"You crazy fucker," muttered Cal in admiration. This guy had real balls. "Come on. We've gotta get out of here."

Between the two of them, Cal and Gaucho helped Daniel up. He was still in pain but regaining his breath quickly. They all stowed their weapons under their shirts and headed back into the hotel as the disposal team went to work taking the body to a inconspicuous drop-off location.

What else could go wrong today?

Chapter 31
Las Vegas, Nevada
3:05pm, September 18th

"**WHAT THE HELL HAPPENED** down there?" Neil blurted as the trio walked back into the suite.

"Someone just tried to take us out," Cal explained. "Please tell me you found out something that'll help us nail these assholes."

Daniel peeled off his Kevlar vest and grabbed some ice as Neil and Cal went over to the bank of computers.

"So, I think we've hit the motherload. These guys are into a whole lot of dirty business. You're not gonna believe how deep this goes."

"Start at the beginning while I grab a drink, Neil. You want one?"

Neil raised a Red Bull and shook his head.

"Okay. Brief overview: Ichiban Gaming is neck-deep into blackmail. It looks like they've got at least twenty Congressman and five Senators in their pockets. Pretty even between Democrats and Republicans. While that may not seem like a lot, they also have over one hundred political staffers under their thumbs. Not to mention lower level government employees. They've got these people on everything from alleged murder to heavy drug use. And that's just the government stuff! I haven't even started pulling out the database of civilians that are on their extortion list."

"So what are they trying to do with all these people?"

"I haven't gotten to that quite yet. My system has to translate everything from Japanese into English. I've probably only uncovered about a quarter of it so far. It'll take some time to unravel."

"Neil, I know I don't need to tell you this, but the shit's about to hit the fan. I'd really like to know more as soon as we can," Cal requested, not unkindly.

"I know, Cal. I'm working as fast as I can. Even my technology has its limits." Neil exhaled in frustration.

"I understand. We just need something we can act on right now. How about you print me off a list of those top politicians so I can take a look. Maybe we can give somebody a heads-up. I mean, I'm not sure how we should handle this information yet. As much as I'd like to make a bunch of Washington-types look like idiots, I'm not so sure America needs that right now."

"Why don't you talk to the Council about it?"

"Our friends are a little busy right now. I think I'll wait until we know a little more about what the exact threat is. Where are Zimmer and Top at?"

Neil pointed up. "I got them a room right above us. Trent's got him cooped up in there for now."

Cal looked over at Briggs. "You good to walk?"

"Yeah. I'll be okay."

"Neil, we're headed up to have a little chat with the Congressman. Can I take those names with me?"

Patel handed him the two sheets of paper and the former Marines headed for the door. Cal had no idea what to do next. There was a large piece of intel they were still missing.

As they reached the stairwell, Cal's cell phone buzzed. It was Captain Andrews.

"Hey, man. Are you here?" Cal could hear slot machines on the other end.

"Yeah. We just landed. You have time to grab a drink?"

Cal glanced at Briggs. "I'm not sure, Andy. I think I'll know more in a few minutes."

"Everything okay?" Andy asked in concern.

"You know me. Never a dull moment."

Andy laughed. "Yeah, don't remind me. All right, give me a call when you know. I have a meeting with the planners at nine, but I'm free until then."

"You got it. I'll talk to you soon."

Cal put the phone back in his pocket and opened the stairwell door.

"Who was that?" Briggs asked.

"Just another Marine buddy. He's a Captain with the Silent Drill Team. Can you believe they're out here to do a show for the Convention?"

"You're kidding me! I thought they only did shows at football games and stuff."

"That's what I said! I guess someone pulled some strings to get them out here. Maybe it'll be..."

Cal stopped when Daniel grabbed his arm. "What if they're part of this?"

"What do you mean?"

"I mean it seems more than a little odd that the Silent Drill Team is performing at a political rally, doesn't it?"

Maybe Daniel's right. But how could they be involved?

"I guess, if nothing else, I can give Andy a heads-up that there could be a threat."

Briggs agreed. "I don't think any of us can be too careful right now."

Cal climbed the last few steps to the next landing and turned to his new friend. "You sure you want to be a part of this mess?"

Daniel grinned. "Are you kidding? I haven't had this much fun since Ramadi."

Cal smiled and clapped the sniper on the back. He'd be a good man to have around. Hell, in the span of less than a week, he'd already saved Cal's life twice. Too bad the man didn't drink or he'd be getting a lot of free booze.

✛ ✛ ✛

They stepped into the suite. Trent and Zimmer were playing cards at the dining room table.

"You want in, Cal?" Trent asked over his shoulder.

"We need to talk." The seriousness of his tone made both men turn.

Cal sat down at the table next to Zimmer. The Congressman glanced down at the sheets of paper. "What's that?"

"Neil hacked into their system. We don't know everything yet, but hopefully we will soon. I need your help, Congressman."

Brandon looked at Cal. It was the first time the Marine had asked him for anything.

"How can I help?"

Spreading the list on the table, Cal explained. "These are the names of other politicians and government employees that the guys behind Ichiban have been blackmailing. Some of them are long-standing. Some are new to the list. The problem is, we don't know what they're being used for."

"I'm still confused. How again do you want me to help?"

"I need you to remember whether this Nakamura guy ever asked you for anything. Did he try to get any information out of you? Did they try to get access to secure files or facilities? Anything out of the ordinary?"

Zimmer sat back and thought about the last six months. At first glance, nothing stood out. He'd thought at the time that Ishi was just working up to asking him something. It always felt like there was a request right around the corner. After all, why else blackmail a Congressman unless you want something in return?

"Not that I can remember. They kept it pretty professional."

Cal knew there had to be a goal. "Did they ever give you anything?"

Zimmer shook his head in frustration. "No. Honestly, I don't remember them trying to manipulate me other than that morning with Beth."

Cal pointed to the list. "Do you recognize any of these names?"

"Of course. Some of them are very powerful men."

"What about a connection. Do you serve with them on any committees? Do they run in the same social circles?"

Zimmer thought for a second. He really wanted to help, but he was the new guy in Washington. He wasn't useful to the old stalwarts yet. "No. I've met the Senators before because of Dad, but I really only know two or three of the Representatives on that list."

It felt like it was just beyond reach.

Daniel interrupted Cal's reverie. "You mind if I take a look at the list, Cal?"

"Have at it."

Cal slid the list across the table. Briggs looked down at the list with Trent. Cal was right. Nothing jumped out. Then an idea popped into the sniper's head: what if it wasn't WHO they were but WHERE they were? Each name had a two-letter abbreviation for the state they served. Daniel scanned the list again, simply focusing on the geographical locations.

The others noticed his increased concentration.

"What do you see, Daniel?" Cal asked.

"I'm not sure, but I think there's a connection with the states these guys represent."

He read the states out loud. "Ohio, Florida, Virginia, Nevada, Iowa, Colorado..."

"Wait a minute," Zimmer interrupted, "those are all swing states!"

Cal looked over at the Congressman in confusion. "Like for the election?"

"I'm not sure about Colorado, but I'm pretty sure the rest of those states are a toss-up right now. But, how could they have known that before the election?"

Cal didn't have a clue, but at least they'd latched on to something. "So you're saying that the Presidential candidates are fighting over these states?"

"Do you ever know what's going on in politics, Cal? Even I know this stuff," Trent teased.

"What can I say? I vote, but in general, politics make me want to throw up. No offense, Congressman."

A week earlier, Zimmer might have fought for his profession. Now, he understood the Marine's point of view. Looking at the blackmail list proved how dirty politics could be.

"Don't worry about it. Right about now it makes me want to puke, too."

The response surprised Cal. Maybe the Congressman really was coming around. He turned back to the list. "Okay, so are we in agreement that these guys might be trying to rig the election?" Nods around the table. "If that's the case, why go to all the trouble? If they want the President to get re-elected, why not just dump a bunch of money into the campaign?"

No one had an answer. What they didn't know was that there would soon be another candidate in the race for President.

After calling SSI headquarters and updating Travis and his staff, the four men walked down to Neil's suite. They were all energized by the recent revelation. These Japanese guys had some balls.

As they walked, one question kept nagging at Cal: *Where was the leak?*

+ + +

The politician smiled into the mirror. Tomorrow would be a very big day. As long as Nakamura kept his end of the bargain, he'd have the election wrapped up in a matter of days.

Chapter 32
Las Vegas, Nevada
3:17pm, September 18th

KAZUO NAKAMURA CALLED the number for the third time. It wasn't like his prized assassin not to check in. Still no answer.

Ishi looked on with interest. For years, Matsura had been a thorn in his side. The man never said much, but Ishi could see his influence growing. Sometimes he felt like his father treated the assassin more like a favored son. Secretly, he hoped the man disappeared.

"Have you tried him again?" Nakamura asked his son.

"Yes, Father. He's not answering calls or texts."

"Maybe he is busy disposing of the bodies."

"I think we need to assume the worst, Father."

Nakamura shot his son a murderous glare. "What do you mean?"

"With all due respect, Father, I think we've underestimated our adversaries again."

"I've sent that man out alone to kill five men at once before! He does not fail!"

Ishi bowed to his father, silently relishing the old man's lack of composure. "I know he has never failed, Father. Maybe he finally met his match."

Kazuo Nakamura paced back and forth, hoping his phone would ring. "We had them within our grasp! We've taken care of the Secret Service and the FBI. How is it that Stokes is evading us?"

Ishi knew he had to steer the conversation back to the task at hand. "Father, tomorrow will be the start of a glorious new path for our people. Perhaps we should focus on that, instead."

His father looked at him with an uncertain gaze. "Of course. Of course, you're right, my son. We must get back to finalizing our plans for tomorrow's festivities."

Ishi nodded and pulled out the chair for his father. Both men sat down and returned to the drawing of the Las Vegas Convention Center.

+ + +

Cal checked the caller ID on the dead assassin's phone. "Same number. Did you get a lock on the signal yet?"

Neil shook his head. "I don't know how they're doing it, but I can't pinpoint where the call is coming from."

"I thought you had that super duper tracking system."

Patel shot his friend an exasperated look. "I do. Problem is, the number isn't registered anywhere. It's like a ghost."

"Maybe I should call him and ask him where he is," Cal offered.

Instead of replying, Neil gave Cal the finger.

"Take it easy on him, Cal." Trent moved closer. "But maybe you're on to something. Hey, Neil, would it help if Cal got the caller on the line?"

"Of course, but once the guy hears it's not the dead dude, he's gonna hang up. I need him on the line for more than a second."

"Maybe Cal can piss the guy off and get him to start talking. How long do you need him on the line?"

Neil wasn't sure. He'd never run into a number that he couldn't track. "I don't know. Maybe thirty seconds?"

Trent turned to Cal. "You think you can get under the guy's skin?"

Stokes grinned. "That's my specialty. Just ask Neil."

Patel gave him the finger again, then refocused on the tracking program.

+ + +

Five minutes later, everybody was ready. Gaucho had two of his four man teams loaded into their vehicles in the parking garage. Neil sat poised at his computer, ready to track the call. Cal picked up the dead man's phone. "Everyone ready?" There were murmurs of assent around the room.

Cal nodded and dialed the number.

+ + +

Nakamura glanced at his phone. The call was from Matsura. He breathed a sigh of relief and answered.

"Where are you?"

"In hell," Cal replied.

Nakamura's eyes went wide. "Who is this?"

"Somebody you don't want to fuck with."

"Where is my employee?"

"Oh, you mean the dead guy?"

Nakamura couldn't believe what he was hearing. Had they really killed Matsura?

"Where is he?"

"I told you. He's probably having a nice little conversation with the devil right now."

"You will pay for this! I will unleash all..."

"Now listen here, asshole. I think it's about time you and I had a little chat. I'm sick of having to kick the crap out of all your goons."

Ishi kept motioning for his father to end the call. The manufacturer had promised it was untraceable, but it was stupid to take the chance. The elder Nakamura ignored him. His pride demanded he confront the cocky American.

"So you are prepared to have me release all our evidence to the authorities?"

"That's where you keep misunderstanding. I could give a shit about a bunch of politicians. Let them fend for themselves. What do you really have? Some pictures of old guys hanging out and talking? That's all retired politicians do!"

Nakamura didn't know how to respond. His contact had assured him that the contents of the envelope would scare off the meddlers.

"I think you are the one misunderstanding me. There will soon be a shift in your puny world. An avalanche is about to cover your little company. I will destroy you."

Cal laughed. "You're welcome to try, buddy. Thing is, next time why don't you show up to the party instead of sending one of your cronies?"

Ishi finally grabbed the phone out of his father's hand and ended the call.

"What are you doing?!" Kazuo Nakamura screamed.

"I'm saving you from making a big mistake, Father. Is it not you who is always telling me to keep my emotions out of business? We are too close to victory to lose our tempers."

Nakamura took a deep breath. His son was right. He wasn't used to having things not go his way. He couldn't remember the last time he'd failed at anything. It was an unsettling feeling.

"I'm sorry, son. Thank you for putting things in perspective."

Ishi nodded and handed the phone back to his father. "Should we go back to our planning?"

Nakamura nodded and returned his attention to the Las Vegas Convention Center diagram.

"Did you get him?" asked Cal, expectantly.

"No."

"What do you mean? I swear I had him on the line for over a minute, Neil."

"I know, but they're using some really new technology. I didn't even get a blip in my program."

"Shit," Cal muttered to himself.

Zimmer walked over to the pair. "Did you really mean what you said about not caring about the politicians?"

Stokes looked into the man's eyes. "We weren't talking about the list, Congressman. It's something else." They'd chosen to keep any talk of the Council away from Zimmer.

"Something you can't tell me about?"

"Yeah."

"Look, I'm in the middle of this thing too. I think you need to..."

Cal's eyes flared. "I think you need to remember that we're here to save YOUR ass, Congressman. The last time I checked, I wasn't the one who got caught with his pants down. Last time I checked, me and my guys are the ones getting shot at. Now, if you want me to lock you in a room until this is over, I'm happy to do it."

"How dare you...?" Zimmer started to respond before Trent stepped between the two.

"Alright, fellas. How about we all take a breather and chill out. I think we could all use a little food and a good stiff drink."

Cal and Zimmer continued to stare at each other. Brandon was the first to walk out of the room, followed by Trent.

Stokes watched the two men go. He couldn't wait to be done with Zimmer.

Chapter 33
Las Vegas, Nevada
4:42pm, September 18th

CAL DIALED Andy's cell number.

"Hey, I thought you would've called earlier."

"Yeah, sorry. Had a little unexpected...incident," Cal explained.

"No problem. You want me to come your way or can you come meet me?"

"Where are they putting you guys up?"

"We're staying at the MGM Grand."

"I'll come see you. Mind if I bring a couple friends?"

"Sure."

Cal woke Brian, snoozing in the recliner.

"Hey, we're going to see Andy." Brian just nodded. "You wanna come too, Daniel?"

"I'm in."

"Alright, let's go in five minutes."

Everyone prepared to leave. They wouldn't be walking the streets of Vegas unarmed anymore. This time Cal and Brian would be bringing their security badges and concealed carry permits. It was one of the perks of SSI's VIP protection division.

Cal knew he was running a risk by hitting the street again, but he had to warn Andy. Besides, he had his lucky charm with him: Daniel Briggs. He'd started analyzing how he could best utilize the sniper in the future. Maybe Briggs would become his vigilant companion like Travis Haden to his father and Todd Dunn to Travis. In his line of work, Cal could never have enough expert warriors around.

Five minutes later, the trio walked out the door. Each one hoped they wouldn't run into more Ichiban goons.

They arrived at the MGM Grand without incident. Instead of trying to take back routes, they'd decided to walk through the most congested public areas. With the Democratic National Convention starting the next day, the sidewalks were overflowing with revelers.

Cal wondered how the convention attendees would feel if they knew about the imminent threat to the big party. It was par for the course and he knew it. Most Americans lived in blissful ignorance knowing nothing about the silent forces of good and evil at work all around them.

Andy opened the hotel room door and invited everyone in. Cal introduced Daniel to the Marine Captain. The two men shook hands and did the Marine size-up.

"Can I get you guys anything?" Andy asked.

"I'd kill for a coffee and a beer," Cal sighed.

"In that order?"

"How about just the beer?"

Andy nodded and took orders from the other two. Once they'd gotten their drinks and taken a seat, Cal told the whole Vegas story to his good friend.

Capt. Andrews didn't interrupt; he just shook his head in amazement time and time again. Cal finally finished. "So I really wanted to make sure you got a heads-up. As you can see, there's some squirrely shit going on around here."

"That's the understatement of the year," Andy commented.

"Have any ideas? Anything we haven't thought of?"

Andy took another swig of beer and contemplated the question. There were too many possibilities to consider.

"I'm just thinking out loud here, but what if it's all a wild goose chase? What if they're throwing you guys red herrings just to keep you away from what they're really trying to do?"

Cal shook his head. "I don't think so. This is shaping up to be something big. We really think the Convention is the trigger."

Andy wasn't convinced. During his time with the Silent Drill Team, he'd seen the capabilities of the Secret Service and the FBI. They'd probably spent months investigating every scumbag in a twenty-mile radius of Las Vegas. These guys knew how to do their homework. The last thing they wanted on their watch was a dead President. There wouldn't be a weapon anywhere near the leader of the Free World.

It was Daniel who broke the silence. "Captain, how about anything out of the ordinary? Is there anything they've asked you guys to do during your routine that you don't typically do?"

"Well, most of our routines are pretty similar. Sometimes our entrance is a little different. Like this time, they're keeping us a secret. You know how they have those big stages for the Super Bowl, where the singer comes up through the floor? Well, they wanted to do that, with a twist."

"What kind of a twist?" Daniel asked, suddenly feeling the hair on the back of his neck stand up.

"They've got this huge trailer that they're gonna pull out. Think of a semi trailer, only like four times as big. So they put us in there, a cannon booms over the speaker system, the sides of the trailer flip down, we're standing there ready to kick ass, and then we march out onto the floor. It's actually pretty cool. We've been practicing it for weeks. We'll have one last run-through tomorrow morning."

They were all impressed. Twenty-four Marines in dress blues made a beautiful sight. The Silent Drill Team as the surprise entertainment would be a big hit.

"Who've you been coordinating that with?" Cal questioned.

"Some woman on the President's event planning staff."

"Do you remember her name?"

"Sure. Janet Riley."

"Why do I know that name?" Cal thought aloud.

"Because she's on the blackmail list," Daniel answered.

Janet Riley, a pretty brunette from Los Angeles, pored over the itinerary for the upcoming convention. Taking the reins in the early spring, Riley brought her Hollywood talent and flash to the President's campaign. Over the past fifteen years, Janet had climbed tooth and nail up the competitive Los Angeles public relations ladder. She'd landed her dream job two years earlier as head of PR for one of the largest studios in L.A. The job included the added benefit of rubbing elbows with some of the biggest influencers in the entertainment industry. During the day she submitted news releases and coordinated publicity for the studio's biggest stars. By night, she networked with Hollywood elite at movie premiers and after parties. She was very good at her job.

It was at one event that she'd met the President's campaign manager. They'd hit it off and kept in touch until the day the campaign needed a new Events Coordinator for the election. She'd worked out a leave of absence from her studio and joined the campaign trail. It wasn't as glamorous as Hollywood, but Janet felt like she was doing her patriotic duty.

Her mind was swirling. She had so many moving parts for the Convention. Sometimes she wondered how she'd be able to keep it all together. To make matters worse, they were doing things a little different this year. Typically, the convention floor was full of constituents for the entire event. For this DNC, the first day would be more entertaining. The lower level would be empty, except for the entertainment and an occasional 'Rah Rah' speech from party leaders. They'd booked three of the President's favorite bands to start. The Marines would really kick things off toward the end of the night. The President wanted the tone to be patriotic, hence the many strings pulled for the Silent Drill Team to perform. In the end, everything would come together. It always did.

Riley looked at her watch. Her stomach grumbled as she thought about the lunch she'd missed and the dinner that would probably also be skipped. She had just a couple of hours before the Marine Corps reps came to the convention center to walk through the space. They'd requested the meeting to finalize the show's particulars. Janet had enough on her plate and wished she didn't have to go. These Marines were perfectionists though. They wanted to make sure every detail was ironed out prior to show time. Riley cursed them and their efficiency.

To make matters worse, the President had just requested to be at the dress rehearsal the following morning before any of the crowd showed. He wanted to see the Silent Drill Team run-through and spend a couple minutes mingling with the Marines. Capt. Andrews would not be happy with the change. At least they wouldn't have to contend with a large Secret Service presence in the morning without a crowd being there.

In another hour, Janet would head down to the convention floor. After that, she'd walk back to the hotel for one final meeting. The guy from Ichiban Gaming had called earlier in the day. He said he had another small request for the convention. Janet wanted to be done with the guy. He gave her the creeps, but she couldn't really deny the request. After all, he had pulled her out of that little situation back in L.A. four months ago. She never should have listened to her girlfriend and gone to that party. Janet knew there would be drugs all over the man's house and she had been secretly battling addiction for five years. In the end, she gave in and got wasted. It was only by a stroke of luck, and the help of that Japanese guy, that she avoided landing in jail.

He'd asked for nothing in return, until two months before the convention. She felt obligated to help because she was in his debt. The request wasn't out of the ordinary. So the guy wanted one of his companies to do some of the work at the convention. Who didn't? It was a big deal to be one of the vendors for a political rally. Besides, the bid was competitive so technically Riley wasn't doing anything wrong. It was her call which companies would be hired to setup for the week's events.

+ + +

Everyone in the room froze. Had they just found a piece of the puzzle?

"Are you telling me that I'm about to go to a meeting with someone on that list?" Andy asked incredulously.

"Looks like it. But the question is, what is she doing to help these guys?" wondered Cal.

"I'm seriously thinking about calling my boss and pulling the plug. Am I the only one that's getting a really bad feeling about this?" Andy asked.

No one answered. They all felt the same way. There was only one direction this was going: downhill.

"Andy, how about you go meet with Ms. Riley and see what you can find out? Who knows, maybe you'll stumble onto something. Who's going with you?"

"My First Sergeant and my squad leaders."

"Good. Starting now, I don't think you or your Marines should be traveling alone. Can you get that word to your men?"

"Sure. I'll call their rooms right now. Anything else?" Andy asked his friend.

Cal couldn't think of anything. "I don't think so. Just keep your eyes open and let us know if you notice anything fishy. Can you give me until tomorrow morning to make the call about cancelling the show?"

Andy wasn't so sure. His sixth sense told him to pack up his boys and head back home. "I guess. But you better be damn sure you're doing everything you can to find out what they're planning."

"We're all over it."

They said their goodbyes and left Andy to make his calls. Cal hoped that they would have a better idea of what they were dealing with by tomorrow's deadline.

"Make sure the Riley woman follows your directions. Remember, we cannot afford another failure."

The Japanese man bowed to his employer. Kazuo Nakamura sat back in his chair as his underling departed. In less than twenty-four hours, everything would change. He looked forward to returning to Japan as a conquering hero.

Chapter 34
Washington, D.C.
8:42pm, September 18th

"**ARE YOU READY** to go, Mr. President?" the head of the Commander in Chief's protection detail asked.

"Sure am." He stretched as he rose from his chair. "Sam, we've really gotta tell the Air Force One boys to stop booking these late flights."

The Secret Service agent chuckled. "Well, sir. You know it makes it a lot easier for the airports when we're not stopping traffic in the middle of rush hour."

"I know. It's just that the kids never get enough sleep when we fly after nine pm. You'd think that after four years they'd be used to it."

"Yes, sir."

The President glanced at his new smart phone and sighed at the time. "Well, I guess we better get going."

He followed his detail out to the waiting caravan.

Chapter 35
Las Vegas, Nevada
8:45pm, September 18th

CAPT. ANDREWS AND HIS small Marine contingent showed up at the Las Vegas Convention Center fifteen minutes early. He'd given word to keep their eyes and ears open without giving details. The Marine Captain didn't look like much to strangers, but his Marines knew the boyish face belied a fearless warrior and strong leader. His gaze remained serious as they toured the staging area.

"What the hell is that?" Andy pointed to the two identical trailers waiting side by side.

"We had to bring in a backup, Captain," answered Janet Riley as she strolled in, hands full of paperwork. "The last thing we wanted was to have the first one crap out and then be dead in the water."

The explanation made sense to Andy. Anytime Marines did a dog-and-pony show for VIPs, they liked to have backups, just in case.

"So which one are we loading into?"

"The one on the right. It's got a small green sticker on it. The backup is on the left with a small red sticker on the entrance ramp."

"Why don't you guys go inspect the trailers while I have a word with Ms. Riley."

His Marines split up and set about testing the mechanics of the two trailers.

"How can I help you, Captain?" Riley asked tiredly. She was ready to wrap the meeting up. It would've been easier for the Marines to just do their inspection without her, but Andrews had requested her presence.

"Are we still a go for the practice run tomorrow morning?" Andy could barely conceal his suspicion of the woman. He wasn't used to holding his tongue. If so much wasn't riding on him to keep his mouth shut, he'd call the woman out right now.

"Uh, yeah, with one change."

Crap. Here we go, thought Andy.

"The President wants to watch the practice run and then come meet your Marines."

It wasn't what Andy had expected. Being part of the world's most famous drill team, he was used to visits by the President and other foreign dignitaries. Considering the strings the White House had pulled to get the Marines there, it wasn't surprising that he wanted to have a quick photo op.

"Alright. I don't think that'll be a problem. Where will he be during the dry run?"

Riley pointed to the far end of the ground floor. "My workers are going to set up a couple of chairs for the President. That's where you guys should finish before you march off, right?"

"Correct. So just forget the about face and march off?"

"If that's okay," Riley requested politely.

The Marines wouldn't mind meeting the President. He was, after all, their President. He wasn't a bad guy and it was rumored that he'd really taken a liking to the Silent Drill Team.

"Sure. If we can make it quick though. I want to get my guys out of their uniforms and taking a break before tomorrow night. We'll be cooped up in that trailer long enough."

"No problem. I think they've only got ten minutes scheduled for that anyway. Anything else I can answer for you?" added Riley, hopefully.

"Not that I can think of. Thanks for meeting us down here. If it's okay, we'll just spend some time walking the arena. You don't need to be around for that."

Riley was grateful. "Sure. Take as much time as you need."

Andy thanked Riley for her assistance and she departed for her room next door at the Hilton. Maybe she'd have a few minutes to take off her high heels before her next meeting.

10:10pm

Andy walked back to his room after a couple of last words with his Marines. They'd all be ready to hop in the vans at first light. The boys knew better than to hit the town tonight. Regardless, he'd passed the word that everyone was to remain in their rooms until the morning. They could party tomorrow night after the show.

He pulled out his phone and dialed Cal.

"Hey, you find out anything?" Cal asked eagerly.

"Not really."

"No changes?"

"Just some minor things."

"Like what?"

"They've got a backup trailer for the show and the President is coming to our practice tomorrow."

"Is that out of the ordinary?" Cal wanted to shut down the show before the Marines were put in a bad situation.

"Not really. It's actually not a bad idea to have a backup trailer. That thing is frickin' huge. We'd be screwed if one of tires went out or the mechanical door stopped working. As for the President visiting, I don't see anything wrong with it. Sometimes the bigwigs want to meet us beforehand because after the real show it's total chaos," Andy answered honestly.

"What about the Riley chick? Was she acting strange?" There had to be something.

"Nope. Looked a little stressed out, but I would be too if I had her job. Sorry I couldn't help, Cal."

"It's not your fault, man. Thanks for keeping this quiet. We'll get to the bottom of it before tomorrow night's show. Wait, do you think you could get me and Briggs and a few other guys in for the practice run tomorrow? I'd like to see the layout and take a look around."

"Let me call one of the Secret Service guys that I just talked to over there. I don't think it'll be a problem as long as you don't come armed and keep your distance from the President."

Cal laughed out loud. "No offense, Andy, but I'll pass on meeting the President."

Andy chuckled. "Cool. I'll call you back as soon as I know."

The call ended and Andy dialed the Secret Service agent's number.

"Hey, Pete. I've got a favor to ask."

+ + +

11:13pm

Congressman Zimmer was just getting ready to hop into bed when his cell phone rang. It was his father.

"Hey, Dad. What's up?"

"Are you ready for the Convention?"

"You still think I should be going with you?"

"Of course. I need you there with me. By the way, there's a slight change for tomorrow. I know I told you we wouldn't need to be at the convention center until five, but I just got a call from the President. He's going to the venue early to watch the Silent Drill Team practice. He invited us to come along to watch and stick around to chat afterward. I think he's going to try to get me to be Secretary of State again. I'll have to tell him no, but you can't refuse a Presidential summoning."

"Why don't you want to be at State, Dad? I thought it was something you'd pushed for before?"

"Maybe with Hank Waller in office, but the current President and I don't exactly see eye-to-eye on much these days. You remember that little argument we had about our CIA assets in Jordan?"

Brandon did remember. His father had grown into a hugely popular figure among intelligence and military personnel. Despite his political affiliation, he was a staunch defender of a powerful armed forces and a robust intelligence arm. The tiff with the President about Jordan had been about the President's decision to pull half of the CIA's human assets stationed there in exchange for a larger drone and signals intelligence presence. Sen. Zimmer had argued that while technology certainly augmented the intelligence gathering process, spies and informants were absolutely necessary. The President, still pushing for full withdrawal from Afghanistan, didn't relent. His closest advisors still professed the increased use of technology because it protected American lives.

Sen. Zimmer almost screamed in the President's face that if it weren't for intelligence community's boots on the ground, Saddam Hussein and Osama bin Laden never would have been found. In the end the President won and twenty-five CIA personnel were pulled out of Jordan. A week later, the coup in Syria caught the American government by surprise. One of the duties of the withdrawn CIA staff was to monitor the situation within the Syrian government. They'd even found seven exiled Syrian officials living in Amman, Jordan, and convinced them to be American informants. Each man still had extensive networks inside Syria. A day before the coup, all seven men disappeared. It was later determined, the lack of American protection around the men had allowed their capture and subsequent murder.

No, Sen. Zimmer would respect the office, but he could not serve directly under the man. Their ideological differences were too extreme.

"So why do you want me to come with you tomorrow?" Brandon asked.

"I think I'm gonna need a little moral support, Son. Besides, it wouldn't hurt for you to mingle with him a little bit. He is the President."

Brandon wasn't sure. He'd have to check with the SSI guys. Then again, what could it hurt?

"Will it be okay to bring Trent with me?"

"Is that your bodyguard?"

"Yeah. It's kinda one of the requirements you signed me up for."

The Senator thought about it for a second. "I don't see why not. I'll call the President's office and have them add him to the list. What's his full name again?"

Brandon relayed Trent's full name and former military rank. What would Trent say about meeting the President?

"I'll have my driver come pick you two up at six thirty."

They ended their conversation with a quick goodbye. Brandon walked into the adjoining living room and found Trent flipping through the TV channels. "Anything good?" Zimmer asked.

Trent answered without looking up. "Nope. It's all commentary on the Convention. This damn TV can't even get me the Falcons game replay."

"Hey, something's just come up."

Trent muted the television and looked at Zimmer. "What's up?"

"My dad got invited to meet with the President tomorrow morning. He wants you and me to come with him."

"What? Cal's not gonna like that."

"I know his attitude isn't your fault, Top, but Cal's being an ass. I don't really care what he thinks right now."

Trent had spent enough time with the Congressman to know that the man had truly experienced a wake-up call. More than anything, the comment was a reaction to his most recent conversation with Cal.

"Congressman, I know you two got into it, but Cal's trying to do the right thing. Put yourself in his shoes. He has to protect you PLUS all the rest of us. All I'm saying is that it's a lot of pressure and you might want to give the guy a break."

Zimmer exhaled. He knew Trent was right. Brandon had grown to respect the SSI men immensely. He trusted their judgment and promised himself that, if allowed to stay in office, he'd never lose that perspective. There were secret men and women, true patriots, that laid their lives on the line so that men like him could do their jobs and America could remain free. It was something he couldn't forget.

"I know," Zimmer replied. "But, this is really important. Have you ever met the President?"

"Nope. They don't let many big dudes like me around the White House, unless you just won the Super Bowl."

"Well, this is your chance. I'm sure Cal will be good with it as long as you're with me. Do you mind asking him? I don't think he's ready to talk to me yet," Zimmer almost pleaded.

The Marine thought about it. On one hand, he was sure Cal would be pissed. It really wasn't smart to let the Congressman out until everything blew over. On the other hand, they'd be surrounded by Secret Service agents AND he'd get to watch the Silent Drill Team. What could go wrong?

"I'll talk to Cal."

"Thanks, Top. You won't regret it," Zimmer smiled.

+ + +

11:47pm

Cal put his phone down and closed his eyes in frustration. Another wrinkle.

"Okay, guys, one more change. That was Top on the phone. Seems as though the Congressman got himself invited to the party. He'll be at the convention center during the rehearsal tomorrow morning, too. I told Top to stick to his ass like glue."

Brian and Daniel looked up from their card game. "So who's going with you tomorrow?"

"Andy called back and said he could only get two passes from the Secret Service. No offense, Doc, but I think I'm gonna take Daniel with me."

Ramirez waived off the apology. "No biggy. That means at least one of us can sleep in tomorrow."

"You cool to come with me?" Cal asked Briggs.

"No problem. I guess we won't be taking any weapons." It was posed as a question.

"Yeah. We can leave them out in the car. I'll bet they'll have that place pretty buttoned up before the big show. I'm more worried about tomorrow night. Why don't you guys hit the sack? I'm just gonna go over that new list Neil gave us. I want to memorize as many faces as I can."

Daniel and Brian finished their game, cleaned up, and went to their rooms. Cal watched them go, wishing he could do the same. It was already midnight. He'd be up for at least two more hours, poring over the files Neil kept digging out of the Ichiban network.

1:25am

Cal had just dozed off when a natty-looking Neil Patel tapped him on the shoulder.

"Hey, what's up?" Cal asked groggily.

"I just found something I think you need to see." The earnestness on Neil's face shook the fuzziness from Cal. He followed Neil to the computer station.

He watched as Neil pulled up a file. "So, earlier I found the original video file of the murder scene. Remember that in the one posted to YouTube, no one else was shown and the girl's face was blurred? Well, this one I'm about to play was put together not only with clips of the Congressman, but also with a full view of the woman's face. You ready to watch it?"

Cal knew they'd find some video like this, so he wasn't sure why Neil was being so damn serious. "Is there something you're not telling me?"

"I need you to watch the video first. Then I'll tell you what it all means."

Cal knew Neil wouldn't waste his time, so Cal nodded to his friend. Patel pressed the Play button.

Cal watched as the cameraman walked around the body. It was similar to the shots he'd already seen online, but this time it showed a full view of the woman's face. She was undoubtedly beautiful. She actually looked peaceful, despite not having any of her limbs attached. *She must've been drugged*, Cal thought.

Next, the camera panned over to Congressman Zimmer. He was lying unconscious, naked, and covered in the woman's blood. The sharp knife had obviously fallen out of his bloody hand and sat inches from his gory appendage.

Holy shit!, Cal thought. He couldn't imagine waking up to that. It reminded him of the iconic horse head scene from *The Godfather*. But this was different. This was a dismembered person. *Maybe I need to cut Zimmer some slack.*

The video finished and Neil looked up at his friend. "So what was your takeaway from that?"

After pausing for a moment to gather his jumbled thoughts, Cal replied. "First thing is maybe we can find out who that girl is. I also just realized Zimmer really went through some crazy stuff there. I'm surprised he's not in the nut house after that."

Neil agreed. Working with SSI, he'd seen some gory crime scenes. This was something different though. You could almost feel the detached brutality and evil of whoever had killed, then cut the poor girl up. It reeked of someone who had absolutely no regard for human life.

"You're right about finding out who the girl was. I ran her through the FBI's facial recognition system..." Neil had a way of hacking into any government agency he needed at the moment, "...and I got a match."

"Just tell me the punch line, Neil," ordered Cal impatiently.

Neil hesitated, "Her name was Patricia."

"I thought Zimmer said her name was Beth."

"Apparently, she wasn't telling him the whole truth."

"What's her last name?" Cal asked, totally intrigued.

"Waller."

"Waller? Is she related to President Waller?"

Neil nodded. "She's his daughter."

"Oh shit!"

Chapter 36
Las Vegas, Nevada
1:30am, September 19th

CAL HESITATED BEFORE grabbing his phone. Who to call first? He was in completely uncharted territory here. Should he call President Waller first? Should he call Travis and get his opinion? His sluggish mind struggled to come to grips with the latest information.

How in the world had she just happened to run into Congressman Zimmer? And, more importantly, why did she call herself Beth? Was she part of a larger Japanese plot?

It was too much for his tired mind to unravel alone. He needed help.

Reluctantly, he grabbed the secure phone and placed a call to SSI headquarters. He asked the man on duty to patch him through to Travis's encrypted line.

Ten seconds later, Travis was on the telephone, voice heavy with sleep. "What's going on, cuz?"

"We just got some news that I don't know what to do with. I need your help."

Travis was suddenly awake. It was rare that his cousin called to ask for anything. This must be big. "What's up?"

Cal told him about Waller's daughter.

"You've got to be shitting me! Have you told him yet?"

"No. That's why I'm calling you! What am I supposed to tell him?"

Travis had no clue. In the military, trained teams were sent to the homes of troops killed in action. Luckily, during his time with the SEALs he'd never had to pull that duty. How in the world do you tell an ex-President that his daughter was murdered and now being displayed all over the Internet?

"This is a big fucking mess, Cal."

"Tell me about it. So what do I do?"

"I think you need to call him and request a meeting right now."

Cal couldn't think of anything better. If it had been his daughter, he'd want to know right away as well.

"Okay, I'll make the call."

"Let me know if you need my help."

Cal killed the connection and dialed Waller's number. He picked up after one ring. Apparently, he was used to calls in the middle of the night because he sounded wide awake.

"Hey, Cal."

"Hello, sir. I've, uh, got some news that I need to share with you," Cal started hesitantly.

"Can you tell me over the phone?"

"No, sir. I think I better head over to your place, if that's okay."

"You think that's safe?"

"I'll bring a couple of my guys with me. If you can just make sure your detail knows we're coming."

"No problem. I'll see you in a few."

The call ended and Cal gazed out the window. He could clearly see the happy crowds enjoying the warm night air, hopping from casino to casino. Cal wished he were with them. Instead, he had to deliver the worst news possible to a President of the United States.

2:13am

He'd woken up Daniel and the two met up with three guys Gaucho sent over. They hurried down to the parking garage and loaded into the rental car. Fifteen minutes later, they arrived outside Waller's hotel. Cal and Daniel hopped out and headed in.

Waller met them at his door and let the two Marines in. The three men were alone, the security detail stayed right outside the suite. Waller's wife was asleep in the adjoining bedroom.

"So what's going on, Cal?" President Waller was in an expensive blue robe. Even past one in the morning, the man looked put together.

"I think we better sit down, sir," Cal requested.

"I take it by your tone and the fact that you've forgotten to call me Hank that this is pretty serious."

Cal merely nodded and took a seat on the large sectional. Waller had weathered more crises than most men will ever have to endure, but the look on Cal's face sent prickles up his spine.

"Sir, we found out who the girl is in Congressman Zimmer's video."

By the look on his face, Waller was starting to put the pieces together. "Just tell me, Cal," Waller asked quietly.

"It's your daughter Patricia, sir."

Waller stared at Cal blankly. He hadn't seen his daughter in almost a year. She'd left for Los Angeles almost three years ago to pursue a career in acting. He and his wife had scattered contact with their only child. In fact, it'd been almost eight months since they'd last talked.

Shortly after arriving in L.A., Patricia had sent her security detail home and refused any more money from her parents. She was going to make it on her own. A part of Hank Waller was proud of his daughter for stepping out and being independent. It was often hard for the children of well-known politicians to have real lives. Waller was happy she'd chosen her own life.

He allowed her to live without the bodyguards, but still secretly kept tabs on her with a private security company. A few months after her independence, he'd received word from the owner of the company that his daughter had fallen in with a disreputable crowd of young actors. All played wholesome characters on TV and film, but in their private lives gorged on heavy drugs and explicit sex. Waller was crushed. He'd thought his daughter would have better sense.

Upon receiving the news, Waller and his wife hopped on a flight to California. They'd tracked down Patricia, who'd by then taken up with a local movie producer twice her age. It was obvious that she'd taken to the drug lifestyle, her skin hanging loosely from her pretty figure. Hank Waller almost cried when she'd first come to the door. He was losing his baby.

Her parents confronted the issue and threatened to have her committed. The intervention hadn't gone well. Patricia stormed out of the house and disappeared. For weeks, the security company couldn't track her down. Then three months later, Patricia had shown up on their doorstep completely out of the blue. She looked clean and healthy. He almost didn't recognize her at first.

She'd grown into a beautiful woman. Hank and his wife cried as they hugged and welcomed her home.

Over lunch, she'd told them the entire story. In short, she'd fallen in with the wrong crowd and allowed them to manipulate her. She was embarrassed but owned up to her shortcomings.

"Most of all I'm sad that I worried you guys," she'd told her parents.

The weekend was perfect. They'd cancelled everything and spent time as a family. That had been eleven months ago. Then she'd apparently gotten a job with a Hollywood PR firm. Traveling extensively, contact had been rare, minus the occasional quick text hello. They'd wondered about the lack of correspondence, but just figured she'd been busy.

Hank Waller put his face in his hands. "How could this have happened?" he asked to no one in particular.

Cal didn't know what to say. Once again, he was in completely unfamiliar territory.

"Is there anything else I can do, sir?"

Waller looked up, the misery plain in his watery eyes. And yet, a spark of anger seethed. "You find whoever did this to my little girl, Cal, and I'll help you destroy them."

2:33am

Cal and Daniel left the President with his quietly sobbing wife.

"You think they'll be okay?" Daniel asked. He hadn't said a word in Waller's posh suite.

Stokes knew Waller was a strong man. You can't be President without having an extra gear. Still, the man was human. He wondered how it would affect Waller's performance at the convention.

"I'll think they'll pull through."

"I'll pray for them."

Cal nodded. He appreciated having Daniel's calming influence around. In response, Cal also said a silent prayer for the Wallers.

3:07am

They finally made it back to the Bellagio after fighting through the drunken crowds. Everyone was headed to the closest food joint before heading in for the night.

"Thanks for coming, Daniel. I'll wake you up in a few hours."

Briggs patted Cal on the back and headed off to get what sleep he could.

Cal took one last look out the large panoramic window. The lights of The Strip shone brightly in the dark desert. He hoped the morning would be uneventful.

The Marine set his alarm and fell back onto the over-sized couch. One of the benefits of his time in the Marine Corps was the ability to sleep anywhere, anytime. Cal was asleep in less than two minutes.

Chapter 37
Las Vegas, Nevada
5:02am, September 19th

THE FIRST SERGEANT had just called Capt. Andrew's room to wake him. Andy kicked his legs off the bed and walked to the bathroom. The details of the day's performance were already aligning themselves in his brain. It would be a very busy day.

5:42am

Cal's alarm went off just as he slipped into one of his recurring dreams. He'd just found out that his parents had died and he was running to the Marine recruiting office. Problem was, in his dream, he just kept running and running. He never got close to his final destination.

He shook his head and looked up to see Daniel sitting across from him, apparently ready to go.

"How long have you been up?"

"Since five-thirty. I'm showered and ready to go."

This guy was good. He'd have to remember that. "Alright, give me a minute to rinse off. You mind making me a cup of coffee?"

"No problem."

Cal trudged off to the spacious bathroom and turned the shower to cold. He needed to shock his system. Today would be a long day and Cal needed a clear head. He held his breath and stepped into the frigid downpour.

5:49am

"Are your men in position?" Kazuo Nakamura asked his compatriot.

"Yes, Nakamura-san. They are prepared to die a warrior's death," the man barked earnestly to his master.

"Hopefully, it will not come to that. We will need many men when we take back the empire. Have you made arrangements for myself and my son?"

The man relayed the plan. Nakamura was satisfied. They would have a front row seat to the coming carnage.

He examined the Nambu pistol in his hand one last time. It was a gift from his father. Somehow, he'd been able to keep it hidden from the authorities. He'd told young Kazuo that the pistol had served him well in the Great War. Many enemies had lost their lives to the simple weapon. Nakamura's eyes flared as he imagined using it against his enemies. Yes, today would be a day to remember.

5:56am

Capt. Andrews looked at himself in the mirror. Even though it could be a royal pain sometimes, he still loved his dress blues. It made him feel like a Marine. As an afterthought, he walked into the bedroom and grabbed the shopping bag Cal's friend Daniel had brought. He'd given it to Andy just before leaving.

"Don't let Cal know, sir, but I thought you might need these."

Andy had looked into the bag, and found a Sig Sauer 9mm pistol, along with two replacement magazines full of ammunition. He silently thanked the sniper for his forethought.

Taking the weapon from the bag, he placed it uncomfortably in his back waistband. There wasn't much room inside the form-fitting uniform, but he didn't care. He wasn't going in naked. Andy deposited one magazine into each of his front pockets.

After looking at himself in the mirror one last time to make sure his weapons weren't obviously visible, he made his way out to the waiting vans.

Chapter 38
Las Vegas, Nevada
6:15am, September 19th

THE MARINES FILED into the convention center, carrying their rifles at port arms. Andy wished they'd been able to bring ammunition for the damn things. He still had a really bad feeling about their upcoming performance. It felt like they were walking into an ambush.

He chatted with the two Secret Service agents at the main entrance, waiting for Cal to arrive. Two minutes later, Stokes walked up dressed in black t-shirt, sport coat, and designer jeans. *So that's Cal's new uniform*, Andy thought. Cal had offered his good friend a position at SSI, but Capt. Andrews wasn't ready to leave the

Corps. He came from a military family. His father and grandfather both retired from the military. Andy figured he would probably stay in for one more tour and then get out. After all, he did have bright prospects as a civilian. SSI was a good place for a warrior to end up.

"Hey, Andy!" Cal called cheerfully, Daniel walking smoothly beside.

Andy handed Cal and Daniel their visitor passes as the Secret Service agents did a quick frisking of both men. "Easy, boys. Your mama know you do that at work?" Cal asked.

The large agent chuckled as he finished frisking Cal with a hard smack on the ass. "Have fun, jarhead."

"Army?" Cal asked the muscular man, rubbing his rear.

"SEAL."

"You know what they say, sailor...?"

"What's that, knuckle-dragger?" the agent asked with a grin.

"What happens in the Navy, stays in the Navy," Cal commented innocently.

The agent's partner laughed and ushered the two Marines into the convention center after taking their cell phones for safekeeping.

Cal and Daniel looked around in amazement. The place was huge. It took them a full five minutes of brisk walking to get to the main event area. They didn't run into anyone else. The convention would kick off a little after 5pm with doors opening at 3pm. It looked like everything was ready and waiting for the impending visitors.

They finally reached the staging area where the Marines were waiting. Cal let them get ready as he and Daniel first examined the trailers and then walked to the entryway leading into the arena. The exhibition space was about the size of a football field. The Silent Drill Team would have plenty of room to maneuver, even with the huge trailer. Cal could make out the short row of chairs on the opposite end of the field where the President would be sitting. He hadn't arrived yet.

Capt. Andrews walked over. "They said you guys can grab a seat on this side of the arena." He pointed right over his head where seating was arranged stadium style.

"Sounds good. What time does the show start?" Cal asked.

"We load into the trailer at quarter 'til seven. They close us in and wheel us into the arena five minutes later. Why don't you guys head up to your seats and I'll see you after the show?"

Andy headed back to his Marines who were carefully being inspected by their squad leaders. They wouldn't be caught dead with even a speck of lint on their uniforms, even if it was practice.

Cal and Daniel took the set of stairs up to the landing where two folding chairs were clearly marked with "Jarhead #1" and "Jarhead #2" written on pieces of white paper.

"Those Secret Service guys sure are funny," Cal noted wryly.

From their seats, they could observe the entire field. It would give them a perfect view. He pointed to the highest point at the opposite end of the arena. They could see the two Zimmers and Trent filing into their row. Cal waved but couldn't catch Trent's eye.

The only thing not in view was the staging area. Little did they know that that was where they should have been looking.

6:27

Trent took the lead as he escorted the Senator and Congressman to their seats. Senator Zimmer had elected to keep his security detail outside. He'd reasoned that the Secret Service would already have the area sufficiently canvassed and secured.

Out of habit, MSgt Trent glanced all around the huge space. He saw Cal and Daniel at the far end of the hall. He waved and Cal motioned back.

Continuing his scan, he looked at the new VIP boxes. He didn't see anyone prepping. Strange. Just as he moved his gaze past the last window, he caught a flicker of movement in the skybox closest to the President. Probably just a cleaning crew, he thought as the figure disappeared again. The Senator was right; the Secret Service should have this place buttoned up tight.

Trent finished his inspection and looked back at the center of the arena. He looked forward to seeing Marines in dress blues again.

✢ ✢ ✢

6:29am

"Get back, you fool," whispered Nakamura harshly to his son. They were comfortably situated in recliners at the back of the skybox closest to the President.

"He didn't see me, Father," complained Ishi. He was getting tired of his father's paranoia. He'd be glad when this day was over.

"That black man looked back this way..."

"But he's staring at the ground floor again, Father. Let's just sit back and watch the show."

Kazuo Nakamura was too close to accomplishing his long-planned mission to relax. His contacts within the ownership of the convention center had paid off. Rather than having a lot of crew prepping the morning of the event, they'd pushed hard to get all the prep work done the day before the event. Nakamura's compatriot who controlled the event coordinator, Janet Riley, had 'requested' that she get the crew out by midnight in order for them to "get rest before the big event." It was a simple request and had seemed reasonable. Riley had complied willingly.

The lack of workers had allowed the Japanese imperialists to stage their people earlier that morning. The absence of building personnel would also mean fewer witnesses.

Better that the American people hear the news on this morning's telecast, thought Kazuo Nakamura. His people would be gone before the authorities had any inkling of the event. Yes, he had planned it perfectly.

6:40am

"All right, ladies, everyone in the trailer," barked the First Sergeant. They methodically walked up the ramp and into the expanded trailer. There was interior lighting, but it was still like walking into a coffin.

Capt. Andrews and the 1stSgt were the last to enter. Andy threw the small Asian crewmember outside the door a thumbs-up and held down the control until the ramp was closed. They were now safely ensconced in the large trailer...or so they thought.

6:43am

The crewman looked around to make sure no one else was around. He was alone. Quickly he typed into his cell phone: *LOAD.*

Ten seconds later, a platoon of seemingly identical Marines entered the staging area from a back entrance. They wore the same uniforms and carried the same M-1 Garand rifles. The only difference was the slightly increased weight of four of the weapons due to the live ammunition inside.

They marched quickly into the backup trailer just as the loud music started booming in the arena. As the ramp door closed, a man in a Marine Captain's uniform turned to the crewmember and snapped a quick salute. The crewmember returned the salute and pulled out a small remote control. He flipped the safety switch and pressed the red button. His duties accomplished, he slipped out a rear exit and drove to the private airfield outside of Las Vegas.

6:45am

Capt. Andrews was giving the Marines last minute instructions when the booming of the convention theme song shook the trailer. "All right, Marines. That music means we have one minute. Right about now, the President is having a seat in the arena. I know some of you guys would love to give the President a hug, but please resist the temptation."

The Marines laughed with their commander as they fixed their bayonets. When the trailer sides flipped down, they'd be arrayed facing out, bayonets at the ready, as if about to ward off a horde of enemies.

"Let's all get into position," the First Sergeant barked over the loud music.

Andy shifted the pistol in his waistband one last time. The damn thing kept digging into his back. *Maybe I was being a little too paranoid*, he thought.

Just as he moved to the center position, the trailers lights flickered. Andy looked up and squinted. Was that steam coming out of the ceiling?

6:48am

"Whew, we just made it," remarked the President.

"Sorry about that, Mr. President. It's Howie's first time in Vegas," the lead Secret Service agent explained jokingly. Howard Grant was the President's driver for the day and a Secret Service veteran of almost twenty years. Contrary to his boss's comment, Grant knew the streets of Las Vegas intimately.

It was actually the President's daughters that had kept them from leaving on-time. They'd insisted on an extended breakfast with Dad. Never one to deny his beautiful girls, the President had relented until his detail leader had discretely tapped on his watch.

The President sat down as the music rose to its first crescendo.

Chapter 39
Las Vegas, Nevada
6:50am, September 19th

THE OVERSIZED TRAILER moved out of the staging area. It paused at the entryway to the arena and waited for the correct point in the music.

+ + +

"Good. They got it to the door. I'd love to see the look on the President's face," Nakamura noted to his son.

Ishi didn't bother to respond. He kept his eyes glued to the arena. Father and son anxiously awaited the show.

+ + +

Half of his Marines were already lying unconscious on the floor.

As Andy had noted the gaseous substance coming out of the trailer's ceiling, he somehow had the wherewithal to take a deep breath. Without opening his mouth, he'd silently tried to gesture to his Marines. His First Sergeant was the first to comprehend and took in a deep breath before the fumes hit.

By the time the mist had moved down past the Marines' necks, some had already collapsed. Andy scrambled to get back to the ramp and engage the opening mechanism. When he got there, the Marine Captain could barely hear his Marines hitting the floor as the powerful gas assaulted their nervous systems.

In the back of his mind, he somehow recognized that keeping his breath in seemed to help. He'd always read that the more powerful chemical weapons entered the body through the skin and not through the airway. Andy had no way of knowing if that were true or not. It was like those videos the government used to show about how to react when a nuclear explosion occurs. Was it real or just made to make it seem that you "could" survive such an event? Was this gas agent the same way?

It had been close to a minute since he'd first inhaled. He pounded on the ramp release button. Nothing happened. He tried again and again then pounded on the ramp itself. Nothing. They were trapped. Almost all of his Marines were on the ground. Through the mist he could just make out his First Sergeant stumbling his way over the platoon of unconscious Marines.

"Looks like they had to go with the backup trailer," Cal noted.

"Huh. Good thing they brought it," Daniel added.

A second later, a cannon in the music boomed loudly and the trailer flaps folded to the ground. The platoon was arrayed in a large oval, some kneeling in the front row, the second row standing; all were arrayed outward with bayonets fixed and presented toward the crowd.

"Wow! That's pretty sweet," yelled Daniel over the music.

Cal agreed. He'd never seen the Silent Drill Team doing anything like this before.

As they watched, the platoon of twenty-four reformed into a column and marched down onto the field.

+ + +

The First Sergeant had finally collapsed to the floor after banging on the ramp with Capt. Andrews. No one was coming to help them. Just as he started to lose his breath, he remembered the pistol in his waistband.

Andy quickly aimed toward the ramp. *Where to shoot?* The mist was clearing so at least he could see where he was aiming. Then he remembered the two hydraulic pumps at the bottom of the ramp that powered the door. Maybe he could shoot them out and push the ramp open. He only had ten rounds in each magazine so he had to be as accurate as possible. Luckily, the trailer sides were made of aluminum instead of steel. At least he'd have a chance. He fired five shots into the bottom of the left side of the door then moved to the right. His lungs ached as he realized he'd depleted almost a minute and a half of air. His limit was fast approaching.

Cal and Daniel watched as the Silent Drill team did its opening tricks in the middle of the field. All of a sudden, he noticed something. "Are those guys all white?" he yelled to Daniel.

Briggs squinted. "Yeah, where are all the black guys? And...wait...are they all Asian?"

Cal's eyes widened as he thought he heard something. He looked at Daniel who suddenly stood up. "Gunshot!" he yelled.

Without another word, the companions ran for the stairs.

The President was enjoying the performance. He loved the Silent Drill Marines. But there was something he couldn't put his finger on. They seemed sharp, but not as precise as he'd seen them perform before. *And I thought they had some African-American Marines*, the President thought privately.

Andy had one more magazine but was out of breath. He shoved the ramp with all his remaining strength. It started creeping open.

Cal turned the last corner and sprinted towards the trailer. He could see a hand sticking out of the side of the door. Daniel joined him as they ran to the trailer and started pulling the ramp down. Simultaneously, they noticed the vapor and quickly held their breaths. Soon the door was open enough that they could pull Capt. Andrews out. He hungrily gasped in clean air as they dragged him farther from the trailer.

Andy pointed back at the chamber. "There's an...emergency release...lever under the...left side of...the trailer that...unfolds the sides."

Cal and Daniel didn't hesitate as they ran back to the trailer to save the other Marines. Holding their breath once again, the two men pulled with all their might on the release lever. They felt a hard click and the trailer flaps started folding down slowly. By the time the flaps lowered, Andy had rejoined his friends.

"We need to get out there and help the President!" Cal yelled over the din. Andy had no idea what Stokes was talking about. He had no way to know about the Marines' imposters. Cal and Daniel bent down and extracted similar objects from their boot heals. Andy couldn't make out what they had in their hands. He followed closely behind Cal and Daniel as they sprinted to the arena.

+ + +

MSgt Trent watched the show silently. Although he'd been impressed by the Silent Drill Team's appearance, the rest of the show seemed a little lacking. He'd have to give Capt. Andrews a hard time about that.

+ + +

The replica Silent Drill Team moved toward the President's position in four precise columns. They'd marched in step until they were twenty yards from the President. On silent cue, the platoon halted and four squad leaders from the rear marched out and to the front of the formation. Instead of doing the standard weapons inspection routine with two pairs, the planners had elected to go with four pairs. The squad leaders commenced the silent inspection, hurling weapons back and forth; making a show of inspecting the barrel and chamber of each gun.

Then, at the same moment, the four squad leaders grabbed the rifles. After doing a precise about-face they kneeled and aimed their weapons at the President. The Secret Service agents barely had time to react as the rounds came downrange.

As the four squad leaders knelt on the ground, Trent sprang out of his chair. He vaulted whole rows as he extracted his pistol from his holster.

He was so intent on the unfolding carnage that he didn't even notice the two politicians following from behind.

+ + +

Brandon caught it a split second after Trent. Without thinking, he followed the Marine, albeit less gracefully. Zimmer was surprised to see his father following, too.

+++

Out of the corner of his eye, Nakamura saw Trent jump out of his seat. "Let's go, Son," he ordered.

"What? Out there?"

"Yes! Now get up!"

Kazuo Nakamura pulled the Nambu pistol out of his coat pocket and walked toward the arena. There were very few people who could ever claim the killing of an American President. Nakamura wanted to be one of them.

+++

Cal, Daniel, and Andy sprinted toward the opposite end of the arena. They could just make out the President and his security team falling to the ground. *Shit, shit, shit*, Cal thought as he ran for all he was worth. He had no idea what they'd do once they got there, especially without weapons, but they'd die trying. The anthem music continued to pound overhead as the three Marines closed the gap. There were twenty-four fake Marines between them and their goal.

+++

Trent fired as he leaped the eight feet down to the arena floor. It wasn't a particularly well-aimed volley, but he centered his front sight post on the mass of men in dress blues. Remarkably, his rounds hit two of the squad leaders and the rest of the bullets flew into the platoon. With twelve shots, he'd incapacitated six men. There were still eighteen men for Trent and his friends to take care of. Trent hit the ground floor and ducked for cover. He quickly reloaded and focused his attention back on the platoon.

Where the hell were the rest of the Secret Service agents?

As they neared the platoon, several of the imposters fell to the ground, clutching wounds. *What the hell?* Cal thought. He ignored his own question and said a silent thanks that the platoon hadn't turned around yet. They were all still oriented toward the President.

He gripped two small composite blades he and Daniel had extracted from their boots. It was a little gift from Neil before they'd left. Patel knew the Marines wouldn't want to go in naked. The small weapons wouldn't do much against ranged weapons, but hand-to-hand they would come in handy.

The three Marines closed the final few feet with only four blades, a pistol with eight rounds, and a pissed off attitude. *Three against twenty-four*, Cal thought, *What else is new?*

He screamed as he pulled the first man back by the head and slit his throat.

After a silent prayer, Daniel followed Cal into the fray. Where Cal was ferocious, Daniel was more methodical as he quickly cut a swath through the crowd. By the time they'd gotten to the middle of the group, the Japanese imposters were refocusing on the pair of maniacal Marines in their midst.

Possibly because of the after effects of the gas or the constricting uniform, Andy couldn't keep up with Cal and Daniel. An experienced triathlete and marathoner, Andy gritted his teeth and tried to move faster. By the time he'd reached the bloody scene, his two companions had already dispatched a good portion of the phonies. The men on the outside of the formation turned inward and leveled their M-1's at the marauding Marines.

Andy screamed in anger and started firing.

Trent cocked his head in confusion as the platoon fell apart and focused their attention inward. *Huh?*

Not one to look a gift horse in the mouth, Trent left his covered position and closed the remaining twenty yards, firing as he ran.

+ + +

Nakamura's eyes widened as he watched his elite guard get slaughtered. It couldn't be. They'd made sure to dispatch the security agents first. Who were these other men?

Ishi answered for him, "It's Stokes!" he yelled, pointing into the chaos.

Kazuo Nakamura growled in rage and ran to the stairs leading down to the arena.

+ + +

Just as he pulled his blade out of another man's brains, Cal felt an excruciating burn along the left side of his torso. He turned just in time to see a Japanese man in dress blues, M-1 Garand aimed straight at him. The man smiled and then the side of his head blew off, instantly killed by the hollow-point round from Andy's weapon.

"Keep moving!" Andy yelled over the booming music.

Cal nodded and looked around. There were only four men left. He finally realized how they'd done it when he saw MSgt Trent pull up. The Marines had no idea why they'd been so lucky.

What they couldn't know was that the squad leaders had been the only ones to be given special ceremonial rounds engraved with Japanese lettering for the WWII era weapons. It was a small vanity that the prideful Nakamura had insisted on, thinking that the one clip per squad leader would be sufficient considering the complete lack of security. He'd underestimated the Marines.

None of the four remaining Japanese had ammunition. If it bothered them, it didn't show. They were standing in a tight formation, bayonets pointed at their enemies.

"Put the rifles down!" yelled Cal at the four men.

Instead of complying, the enemy on the far left yelled something in his native tongue. His warriors charged.

Kazuo Nakamura peeked around the corner. He watched and smiled grimly as his four remaining loyalists charged. It would be an honorable death.

As quickly as possible, he made his way to the American President, pistol at the ready.

+ + +

They were out of rounds. Just like their ancestors at Belleau Wood, the trenches of Okinawa, and the jungles of Vietnam, the four Marines moved to meet their enemy.

+ + +

Congressman Zimmer climbed down to the ground floor. His father had opted to take the stairs. He ran toward the prostrate President, not realizing the Nakamuras were stalking in right behind him.

+ + +

The eight men met in a clash of steel and flesh. Both sides were highly trained and deadly. The hulking Trent was the first to dispatch his opponent by dodging the man's bayonet stab and then the butt of his empty pistol onto the top of his opponent's head. The powerful blow crushed the man's skull and he collapsed to the ground. Trent turned for a new target.

+ + +

Andy wasn't so lucky on the far right. Still woozy from the trailer episode, he just missed a parry and got a nasty cut deep into his forearm. The assailant kept stabbing, trying to gut the Marine Captain. All Andy could do at the moment was dodge the stabs until there was an opening or the challenger overcommitted.

✚ ✚ ✚

In the middle of the group, Cal picked up a bloody Garand rifle from the ground and charged his foe. The two adversaries thrusted and parried. Taking a step back, Cal flipped the rifle over in his hands and gripped the weapon like a baseball bat. With tired arms screaming in protest, he swung the butt end of the rifle at his rival's head. The man scrambled to bring his own rifle up vertically to block the swing. He never had a chance. The swing was too powerful. The Marine was too mad. The stock of the M-1 blew through the parry and smashed into the man's head. Game over.

✚ ✚ ✚

Next to Cal, Daniel surprised his foe by throwing one of his knives straight at the man's face. It was a pretty harmless throw, and Briggs would've been lucky if the thing had done any damage. But that's not what he wanted. The Japanese raised his rifle to block the projectile. He heard the satisfying clang as the weapon bounced off harmlessly. However, this action gave Daniel the distraction he needed. Going to the ground, he did a quick roll and thrust his remaining blade into his target's abdomen. The man dropped his weapon and grabbed his stomach. Daniel extracted the dagger and drove it up through the man's throat. He gurgled as the sniper twisted the blade through the man's neck. The imposter fell to the ground, dead.

+ + +

Andy was struggling to keep up with his enemy's thrusts. He'd gotten two more deep cuts on his arms trying to deflect the longer bayoneted rifle. Out of the corner of his eye, he saw Trent step behind the remaining Japanese soldier.

The lone warrior noticed Andy's glance and turned to face his new threat. Too late. Like an anaconda, Trent's enormous arm wrapped around the man's throat and squeezed. The man dropped his rifle and scrambled to tear the giant's grip off his windpipe.

Before he could do so, MSgt Trent twisted the man's head violently and severed his spine. He discarded the imposter on the ground.

In unison, the four Marines turned toward the President. They saw Brandon Zimmer bending down to check on the American leader. They also noticed the two Japanese men approaching the Congressman from behind.

Chapter 40
Las Vegas, Nevada
7:01am, September 19th

BRANDON ZIMMER BENT down to check on the President. The leader of the free world moaned and rolled over, gripping his left arm. He was alive! Wounded, but alive.

"Hold on, Mr. President, I'll help you get your arm wrapped."

"What...where are my...?" the President tried to ask.

"Let's just get you out of here first, Mr. President," Zimmer yelled over the music that still reverberated loudly overhead.

The President grimaced as he tried to sit up. Brandon couldn't believe he'd survived the firing squad. He got the President to his feet.

"Walk away from the President!" yelled a voice behind him.

He turned to find Ishi and his father walking closer. The elder Nakamura was pointing a small pistol right at Brandon.

"Fuck you!" Zimmer yelled as he stepped to shield the President. Kazuo Nakamura changed the angle of his weapon and shot the Congressman in the leg. Brandon fell on top of one of the dead Secret Service agents and screamed, clutching his shattered patella.

Cal and his three friends stopped short when Zimmer was shot. They were four men against two, but Nakamura was the only one with ammunition. He saw Senator Zimmer at the entryway, opposite the Japanese. Cal motioned for the Senator to stay where he was. Richard Zimmer ignored the hand signal and walked purposefully toward the President.

As if on cue, the music overhead ended. The four Marines poised to make a run for the President. Kazuo Nakamura leveled his weapon at the President and addressed his adversaries. "If you want the President to live, you will stay back."

They didn't doubt him.

Senator Zimmer approached the President from behind and put his right arm around his boss' opposite shoulder. "How are you, Mr. President?"

"Zimmer? What...what's going on?" asked the President in confusion.

In response, Senator Richard Zimmer pulled a pistol out of his left coat pocket. "Well, Mr. President, I hate to tell you that this will be your last day in office."

"What are you talking about?"

"Well, let's just say I'm sick of your pansy-ass. I think it's time for a new world leader."

The President looked at the head of the Senate Intelligence Committee in shock.

"Don't look so surprised, Mr. President. It's truly unbecoming of an American President to be so afraid of death."

The President steeled his gaze. "You'll never get away with this."

Sen. Zimmer chuckled. "That's where you're wrong, as usual, Mr. President. You see, by the time the smoke settles, all of you will be dead and I'll be the last one left. The Party and Americans will flock to me in their grief. Losing an American President is a small price to pay for getting our national pride back."

Before the President could respond, Kazuo Nakamura cut in. "Enough of this, Senator. Let me kill him so that we can catch our flight home."

Richard Zimmer looked back at Nakamura with barely disguised contempt. Yes, he had been useful, but maybe it was time to end their relationship. He leveled his gun at the Japanese businessman. "I think maybe I can do this without you now, Nakamura-san." Without another word, he aimed at Nakamura's son and fired two rounds. The bullets slammed into Ishi's chest.

"Father..." he said quietly as he reached for his father, instead falling to the ground.

"You will pay for that..."

"Oh, what are you going to do? Shoot me with that shitty little Nambu? Did your father give you that before he died, Kazuo?" the Senator asked, smirking. He knew all about Nakamura's familial past.

"How dare you...?" seethed Nakamura.

"Oh shut up, you Nip. Did you really think that I was going to let you build your little empire? You've got to be fucking kidding me. If I'd known..." Zimmer stopped talking as he noticed Nakamura laughing almost uncontrollably.

Zimmer's face colored. "What are you laughing at?!"

Nakamura continued to howl crazily. Everyone watching thought the man was cracking up. Finally, he quieted and looked back at his mole in the American government.

"I'm laughing because I read you so well, Senator."

"What are you talking about, you idiot?"

"I knew you would double-cross me. Yes, you've become a very upstanding public figure in the last twenty years. But does anyone remember your early days? The days when the Irish mob bankrolled your election? How many favors did that cost you? And only to have that same mob investigated and put in jail years later. Tsk, tsk. No, Senator. You and I are more alike than you might think," Nakamura smiled.

"I am nothing like you. You know what, I'm done..."

"No, Senator, I have one more surprise for you."

Zimmer looked back in confusion. He thought he covered his bases. *What does this little Japanese prick have up his sleeve?*

"While you were so concerned with weaving your little plot to take over the Presidency, we were quietly making deliveries to your beloved Representatives."

"I have no idea what you are talking about," replied a flustered Zimmer.

"We know about the new Opel smart phones that everyone wants. You Americans will soon wait in line for days for this little piece of technology," Nakamura held up his own Opel smart phone. "You know that we've established a large network of blackmailed American government officials over the years. Well, our experts in Japan were able to acquire a single shipment of phones and retrofit them with a little gift."

Zimmer's eyes narrowed. "This was your insurance policy?"

"Yes, now you understand! You see, if my son and I don't arrive for our flight in thirty minutes, my people are ordered to detonate the devices," Nakamura said smugly.

"Detonate?" Zimmer asked.

"Why, yes. My staff is very crafty when it comes to technology. What you don't know is that we've been secretly developing a higher grade of explosive that is undetectable by scanners or your bomb dogs. Quite impressive, really. This explosive was inserted with remote detonating software onto the Opel smart phones. We've already confirmed delivery to over one hundred of your Senators and Congressmen. There are also over two hundred other important business leaders and government workers who received the phone over the last two days. They were very happy to get an early version of the phone. In fact, if I'm not mistaken, even the President has one of our phones in his pocket. Now, I'm not sure, but wouldn't it be difficult to be President and run a country without half of your elected officials? Not to mention all the businesses that would suddenly be without their leadership."

"You son-of-a..."

"Let's not call each other names, Senator. Why don't we just finish our business and move on to more glorious times for both of our countries?"

"So what are your terms?" Zimmer asked through gritted teeth. He'd hoped to be rid of the Nakamuras and not have to follow through on all the silly promises he'd agreed to.

"Simply this: I kill the President, all his friends over there..." he motioned to the four immobile Marines, "...and I walk out of here with my son."

"What about my son?" Zimmer asked, warming to the idea.

"Take him with you, as long as you think he can keep his mouth shut."

"I'll take care of my son. How do I know that you won't detonate those phones if I let you go?"

"You don't. But it would be much better for me to run the new Empire of Japan with the help of a healthy American ally. Besides, I'll be more than happy to give you a detailed list of all the recipients of our...upgraded phones once we land in Tokyo."

"What am I supposed to do with this mess?" Zimmer motioned to the piles of dead men.

"We'll use the same story we agreed upon. Those men were a rogue terrorist unit aligned with the growing Chinese communist threat. My government will be very apologetic and supply information corroborating your claims. We already have the documentation produced. It will all be taken care of."

The senior Senator from Massachusetts wasn't sure, but he didn't have much choice.

"Okay. If your son is still alive, take him and..."

His comment was cut short by six loud gunshots from the handgun Congressman Zimmer had taken from one of the dead Secret Service agents.

Kazuo Nakamura looked down at his pockmarked chest and dropped his pistol. Very slowly, he gazed up as blood seeped out of the corner of his mouth. His final mumbled comment, as he fell dead, was muffled by Ishi's crying.

"What have you done, Brandon?" Zimmer asked his son in shock.

"I was sick of listening to the little fucker."

Brandon struggled to stand on his one good leg. He managed to get up and face his father and the President. The Senator's pistol was pressed to the side of the President's head.

"What now, Dad?"

"Shoot him."

Brandon raised his gun and fired two shots.

Chapter 41
Las Vegas, Nevada
7:11am, September 19th

THE SENATOR'S LIFELESS BODY crumpled to the floor as Cal rushed to help the President. He looked up at the Congressman in surprise. "How'd you learn to shoot like that?"

"Didn't I tell you that Dad made me join the Yale pistol team?" Zimmer deadpanned. He still couldn't believe he'd done it. He'd killed his own father.

Cal shook his head in wonder as his friends surrounded the President. "Mr. President, would you mind if I borrowed your phone?"

The President looked embarrassed that he'd forgotten the small bomb in his pocket. He carefully extracted the phone and handed it to Cal.

Stokes grabbed the Opel phone and dialed a number from memory.

"You think you should do that, Cal?" Brandon interrupted.

"You heard what the man said, Congressman. We have almost thirty minutes until this sucker explodes." He turned his attention back to the phone and dialed a number from memory. The other end picked up after the first ring. "Neil, we have a problem."

Chapter 42
Las Vegas, Nevada
5:00pm, September 19th

THE FIVE FRIENDS SAT on the large couch and watched the kickoff of the Democratic National Convention. Within a minute, Neil was snoring soundly.

"Poor guy. He's been up since we got here," Brian observed.

Cal yawned and went to stretch before remembering the stitches in his side. "Son-of-a..."

Everybody that was awake chuckled. Cal looked around the room, still amazed that they'd all made it. It had been a close call, but in the end, the technological genius of the imperialist Japanese hadn't come close to matching the skill of Neil Patel. Rather than search through the haystack for the trigger, Patel simply wiped out Ichiban's entire system. He had, of course, already made a copy of all the files for future use. For now the threat was no more.

With the help of the President's phone call to the Japanese Prime Minister, all of Nakamura's associates were being rounded up as they arrived back in Japan. In Las Vegas, the Secret Service gathered up the Russian clan under Japanese contract. Rather than postpone the convention, the President was patched up, the convention center cleaned, and the show continued.

It was decided between Zimmer, the President, and Cal that allowing the convention to run as planned would be what America needed. Cal had to give the President credit. Rather than use the whole episode as a stepping-stone in the election (if the entire plot got to the public, they were all sure the incumbent would receive more than his fair share of sympathy votes), he chose to direct the Secret Service to keep the whole thing quiet. They'd mourn for the dead soon.

It was also agreed that certain stories would be concocted for the various deaths and injuries the team had endured. The President would pretend that he'd fallen and dislocated his elbow while dancing with his little girls. Congressman Zimmer, who received a personal invitation by the President to sit in his skybox, would tell his staff and the media that he'd shattered his knee mountain biking.

The Opel smart phones were also being quietly "recalled" through coordination with the FBI.

To further show his gratitude, the President agreed to let the Silent Drill Marines skip the convention. They'd all regained consciousness almost an hour later. By that time, the arena had been cleansed by the Secret Service and the Marines were moved to a new location in another part of the convention center. It was explained that an exhaust valve had leaked and rendered them all unconscious. The Marines were all smart enough to realize they'd never smelled anything like exhaust, but let it go when they were carefully warned by Capt. Andrews not to say anything about the incident. It hadn't hurt that the President had stopped by and apologized for the malfunctioning trailer.

As for Senator Zimmer and the Nakamuras, Ishi died just before Neil killed the Ichiban network. He never uttered another word as he watched Brandon help coordinate the cleanup. Ishi's body was later disposed at a local crematorium. Senator Zimmer and Kazuo Nakamura were transported by SSI personnel to a local pet crematorium. Their ashes were already scattered to the desert wind.

Just before he went into surgery to have his knee repaired, Congressman Zimmer chose the story to end his father's life. He was lucky to have a team of top orthopedic surgeons flown in by the President.

He whispered it to Cal just as the Versed started to kick in, his smile giving away his drugged state. "Tell the media that my Dad died humping a hooker."

Cal snorted as they wheeled the Congressman back to the operating room. Maybe that guy wasn't so bad after all.

He made a call to Travis and floated Zimmer's idea.

"How about we just tell them he had a heart attack?" Travis offered.

"Sounds good."

Cal hung up the phone and wondered what would've happened if they really had leaked the hooker story.

+ + +

Ten minutes later, Cal's cell phone rang.

"Hello?"

"Hey, Cal, it's Brandon."

Before his surgery, Congressman Zimmer had made Cal promise that he'd call him by his first name.

"Hey, man. How ya feeling?"

"Anesthesia's almost worn off and they've got me on some good pain meds. Can't feel my leg, so that's good."

Zimmer paused as he fought for the right words to say.

"Cal, I just wanted to thank you again for all that you've done. I...I don't know what would've happened if you hadn't been there."

"No problem. That's our job, remember?"

"Yeah, I know, but I was a real..."

"Don't worry about it. Trust me. I'd have been surprised if you hadn't been an ass when I first met you.

You would've made me feel bad about talking so much crap about your political affiliation."

Zimmer chuckled and paused again. "Cal, I...uh...was wondering if you could do me one more favor."

"What's that?"

"I was wondering if you could go with me to see President Waller."

Chapter 43
Las Vegas, Nevada
11:36pm, September 19th

PRESIDENT WALLER ENTERED his suite and stared at the two guests sitting in his living room.

"Will there be anything else, Mr. President?" his Secret Service agent asked.

"No, we're good Kurt. Thanks."

The imposing bodyguard nodded and walked out of the room.

"Thanks for waiting for me, gentleman," Waller said stiffly, "the President wanted to have a word with me."

He walked to the wet bar and chose a bottle of Jack Daniels. After pouring himself half a tumbler, straight up, he headed over to the leather sectional and took a seat.

"What did you want to see me about, Congressman?" Waller asked impatiently.

Brandon had thought about what he would say to the father of his murdered lover. What could he say?

"I...I just wanted to say I'm sorry...and that if you want me too...I'll turn myself in to the authorities," Zimmer stammered uncharacteristically.

Waller sighed and his face softened. "Now, why in the world would you want to do that?"

"I just thought that after what happened to Be...I mean, Patricia..."

"Let me stop you right there. First, you were both consenting adults. Second, the fact that she was being used as a pawn by that Japanese murderer..." his eyes hardened then mellowed again, "...it wasn't your fault, son."

"I know, but I keep thinking that if I'd recognized her or if..."

"Don't talk about what ifs, Brandon." Waller said in a fatherly tone. "Patricia was a big girl. She made her own decisions. There's no way you could've known who she was. She'd changed a lot since my days in the Oval Office. Besides, I'm guiltier than you are in this whole thing."

"Why is that, sir?" Zimmer asked in bewilderment.

"Well, I'm guilty for not keeping a better eye on my little girl. I got too busy and didn't follow up like I should have. If I had made the effort of spending more time out west, I'm sure I'd at least known SOMETHING was going on. But more important to this discussion, I'm guilty of leaking our organization's existence to your father."

Cal, with Waller's permission, had already told Zimmer about the Council.

"Now, sir, I don't know how..."

Waller held up his hand. "Let me finish. Once Cal told me it was your father who was scheming for the Presidency, all the pieces fell into place. I remember every conversation I had with Richard. I'm the one who gave him the opening. I'm the one who almost got us all thrown in jail. So you see, it's really up to YOU whether I should turn MYSELF in."

Cal and Brandon stared at the man in complete shock.

Cal broke the silence. "Mr. President, you know that I would never..."

"It's okay, Cal," Waller soothed, "I know you'd never turn me in. It's one of the things about you and your guys. Dependable to the last man. You would never expose a secret operation. I only wish we had more men like you. So, I guess the ball's really in the Congressman's court, isn't it, Brandon?"

Zimmer didn't know what to say. He'd come here hoping to apologize and dreading the possibility of going to jail. Now, a former President was asking HIM if HE should go to jail.

"Mr. President, if there's one lesson I've learned through this whole ordeal, it's that there's a reason for secrets. I didn't know how important it was until this week. It's also imperative to have men like you and Cal fighting the good fight, taking it to the enemy day-in and day-out. I never understood that before. Call it ignorance maybe. I don't know. But my eyes have been opened to a whole new reality. I only hope that I have the chance to go back to Washington and do what's right for this country."

Epilogue
Camp Spartan, Arrington, TN
9:47am, September 24th

CAL AND DANIEL ROUNDED the last bend and slowed their pace down to a jog.

"How's your side feel?" asked Briggs.

The doctors had told Cal not to excercise for two weeks because of his stitches, but he just had to go for a run and get the crud out. His wound was burning, but his body felt great. He hadn't had a chance to work out in weeks.

"It's okay. Just feels good to get out on the trail, you know?"

The sniper nodded, barely even winded.

"Hey, I'm gonna go over to the barracks and get cleaned up. Wanna meet for lunch at eleven?" Daniel asked.

The day after the convention massacre, Briggs accepted a position at SSI. He hadn't even hesitated as Cal extended the invitation and a handsome compensation package. Internally, Daniel was overjoyed. His prayers had been answered and he'd found a new home.

His duties weren't completely ironed out yet, except for being Cal's constant companion, but the sniper was already making a name for himself on the live fire range. The operators around the campus all started calling him Snake Eyes.

He'd made one request as they'd said their goodbyes to the President in Las Vegas: that the President stop the processing of his Medal of Honor. Daniel still felt as if he didn't deserve it. The President finally acquiesced. Two days later, a small package arrived at Camp Spartan for SSI's newest employee. Daniel opened the box and found a Medal of Honor along with a note from the President. It read:

"Sgt. Briggs, I understand your reasons for not wanting this medal, but I must tell you that you are wrong. You are a hero to this nation and your sacrifices will always be remembered. I will keep my promise and not publicly give you this award. But, I did think that you should have this from a very appreciative Commander in Chief and a grateful nation. Semper Fidelis and God Bless."

He'd only shown it to Cal who nodded and patted his friend on the back. As a Navy Cross recipient, Stokes knew how Briggs felt.

"Yeah, I'll see you there at eleven," Cal replied.

Daniel broke off towards the barracks and Cal continued on.

Winding up by The Lodge, a large log cabin style hotel for visiting VIPs, Cal noticed a black SUV parked out front. He wasn't expecting any company.

"I wonder who that is," Cal thought out loud.

He sprang up the steps and headed for his room on the second floor. It was great not having to drive to work. Before he got to the bank of elevators, he heard someone call his name.

"Cal!"

He turned around to see Congressman Zimmer, leg braced and walking with a cane, coming his way.

"Hey, Brandon, what are you doing here?"

"You know, I thought I'd stop by while I was in the neighborhood."

Cal laughed. "Seriously, what are you doing in Nashville?"

"I was wondering if we could have a little chat."

"Sure. You mind coming up to my room?"

They talked about how the Congressman's rehab was going and Cal bitched about his stitches while they rode the elevator and then walked to Cal's suite.

Cal held the door for Zimmer.

"Wow! Nice place you've got here," Zimmer admired as he looked around.

"Yeah. One of the perks of being an owner, I guess." Never one to beat around the bush, Cal dove right in. "So, how can I help?"

Zimmer winced as he took a seat on the closest chair. "Well, there've been some developments in my political career," he said cryptically.

"Don't tell me there's another psychopath trying to blackmail you!"

"Nothing that much fun. No, I've been approached by the Democratic Party to run for my dad's open Senate seat in Massachusetts."

"Well that's great, isn't it?"

"Sure, but it's not a given. I'll have to run in a special election. I'm so young that I don't know if I'll win."

"What's the worst that could happen, you still get to be a Congressman?" Cal joked.

Zimmer laughed. "Yeah, I know. But I'm just not sure if I'm qualified."

"I don't mean to repeat myself, but how again do you need my help?"

"I wanted to ask you, as a friend, whether you think I should run for Senate."

Cal was floored. *Why is he asking me? How am I qualified to give that kind of advice?*

"Look, Brandon, you know I stay way outside the political stuff. I wouldn't know the first thing about..."

"I guess I'm just asking if you think I have a shot."

Cal looked at his newest friend. They had been through a lot. He wondered how else the universe could've thrown the two men together.

"In my humble, dumb grunt opinion...I think you should do it. I mean, you're not half the asshole your dad was."

They both laughed at the macabre reference.

"Okay. Thanks, Cal."

"No problem. But, I'm sensing there's something else?"

"There is. I've been invited to a new club."

"What, like Army-Navy?"

"No. President Waller has asked me to be a part of the Council of Patriots."

Cal couldn't conceal his surprise. "I don't understand."

"Well, Waller figured that I already know about it and now I'm in a better position to help. He's even gonna quietly put his political backers behind my run for Senate."

"But, all the members are RETIRED politicians. Isn't that putting you in a precarious position?"

Zimmer was suddenly serious. "Two weeks ago, I had a really different view of how the world works. Now I know that groups like the Council exist for a reason. They're part of the solution not the problem."

"And you're okay with the way we go about exploiting the intel we get?"

"You're really asking ME that?" Zimmer asked with a sad grin. "Have you already forgotten what I did in Vegas?"

Cal would never forget Zimmer shooting his own father in the face. He was still surprised that it had been the Congressman who had killed the two masterminds of the conspiracy.

"Alright, alright. I get it. So, that brings us back to the original question: how can I help?"

"I've been tasked by the Council to bring you this." He handed over a single sheet of paper.

Cal skimmed the summary and looked up.

"Anything else I should know before we start looking into this?"

"President Waller figured you'd want to do some research first. How about we…"

The two turned as a loud ringing sounded in Cal's makeshift office. "Sorry, that's my secure line. Let me go grab that."

Stokes trotted over to his small desk and picked up.

"Stokes."

Zimmer watched as Cal's face went blank.

"Are you sure?" His face gave away his total shock. "Okay, I'll be right over."

Cal hung up the phone and didn't say a word.

"Is everything alright, Cal?"

"No." Stokes answered as he rhythmically clenched and unclenched his fist.

"What happened?" Zimmer asked with concern. He'd never seen the normally unflappable Marine in such a state.

Cal turned to the Congressman with dread-filled eyes.

"Neil's disappeared."

Thanks for reading *Council of Patriots*. If you liked the book, please take a minute and write a review on Amazon. Also, please consider sharing this book with your friends via email and social media.

To hear about new books first, sign up to my **New Release Mailing List** at www.CorpsJustice.com.

Follow us on Facebook at
http://www.facebook.com/CorpsJustice

Thanks to my editing staff:

Katie, Kevin, Scooter, Chuck, Eric, Brian, Dave, Mitch, Don and Anne

Questions For The Author?
Email me at Carlos@CorpsJustice.com

SEMPER FIDELIS

64861726R00172

Made in the USA
Columbia, SC
12 July 2019